BEST
WOMEN'S EROTICA
2015

BEST
WOMEN'S EROTICA
2015

Edited by

VIOLET BLUE

CLEiS
PRESS

Published in the United States by Cleis Press Inc.,
an imprint of Start Midnight, LLC,
609 Greenwich Street, Sixth Floor, New York, New York, 10014.

Printed in the United States.
Cover design: Scott Idleman/Blink
Cover photograph: Novastock/Getty Images
Text design: Frank Wiedemann
First Edition.
10 9 8 7 6 5 4 3 2

Trade paper ISBN: 978-1-62778-088-9
E-book ISBN: 978-1-62778-103-9

"More Light," by Laila Blake, was previously published in *Best Erotic Romance 2014*; "The Kissing Party," by Rachel Kramer Bussel, was previously published in *Bound for Trouble*; "The Seven Ravens," by Ariel Graham, was previously published in *A Princess Bound*; "Postcards from Paris," by Giselle Renarde was previously published in *Slave Girls*. All published by Cleis Press.

CONTENTS

INTRODUCTION:
DIAMONDS ARE BETTER

This being my tenth year of editing the *Best Women's Erotica* series, I naturally looked up what the traditional wedding gift would be after crossing the threshold of ten years of hot sex, an online sexual revolution for women and porn, and a growing readership spanning digital divides.

Image my disappointment when I found out the gift for a decade of bliss was tin.

This is what we get for slogging through all that bad erotica, packed with gross puns, puerile poetry, and twenty-page *"Penthouse* Letters"–style porno in pink Comic Sans? After going beyond "keeping the spark alive" to showcase women's fantasies about fucking as they transcend into literary supernova territory? We get a bendy pie plate?

Luckily, Hallmark had the foresight to take this dubious tradition and upgrade it. Now, they say, it's diamonds for a ten-year marker. Phew.

And what a glittery jewel box is in 2015's haul, dear reader.

My voyeur and I had never met in person, but he was the one who came to mind whenever someone asked if I had a boyfriend. Our arrangement had lasted five years by then. Every couple of months I traveled for a weekend to a town I didn't know and gave Ron hints about where I'd be. He always sent me the pictures afterward, and it made me feel like a celebrity to sit down at my kitchen table at home and deal out the glossy eight-by-ten prints he'd made of me, some in color and some in black-and-white. He usually caught some shots of me getting undressed before bed, sliding my panties down my thighs, but others he grabbed while I was out doing seemingly ordinary things, crowning me with unexpected sexiness. The pictures were erotic but generally not explicit, and more than once I'd caught myself wondering how my pussy would appear under his lens.

—"Click-Click-Click," Annabeth Leong

A question I'm often asked after over a decade of editing explicit erotica and running an adults-only blog is, "Don't you get tired of erotica? Haven't you seen it all by now?"

The long answer is a languid story about a confectioner who never tires of her luscious, sweet creations and the songs they sing on her tongue and the palates of others. It stars a heroine-as-reader (that's you), who is more afraid of a life less lived than of swimming into uncharted erotic waters. At the end, she realizes there is no such thing as having "seen it all" and that's so delightful and powerful and freeing that none of us want to stop looking for the next delicacy, the next unknown taste, and in this case, the next erotic adventure put to page by a woman as daring as we all strive to be.

The women in *Best Women's Erotica 2015* are these very women, and their compelling, surprising, skillfully told, ridiculously sexy stories star erotic heroines that I guarantee will have you holding your breath before you turn the page—no matter how many servings of erotica you've sampled.

> He described how Rebecca shared him with the CEO of a petroleum company in a hotel suite, Giles stripping for the two of them and sliding his hard cock in the CEO's mouth.
>
> "It's irresistible when someone knows what you want before you do," he said. "You wonder what else they know about you. They become your sexual oracle."
>
> "Did she? Know what else you wanted, I mean?"
>
> "Of course. The first time she tied me up, I thought I would explode. The absolute powerlessness and fighting her authority—then succumbing to my own need for that powerlessness, which is the true humiliation."
>
> Recognition flooded my face in a warm blush. I tilted my head so that my hair covered my cheeks.
>
> "I see that's how it is for you," he said.
>
> I laughed nervously. My legs felt weak and my underwear was wet.
>
> "I'll show you."
>
> —"The Ghostwriter," Valerie Alexander

Finding these gems wasn't easy. As with every year, during an open call of only four months, I read hundreds (this year, again over three hundred) of submitted stories that had never been published, most written in the express hope of being published among the eighteen finalists here.

Not satisfied that I'd turned over every rock trying to find the best, I also read everyone else's erotic anthologies and collections claiming to have "the best"—and shook down editors everywhere to tell me about the hottest stories they'd read all year. When I found new stories that shined beyond the rest in other people's collections, I plucked them like a greedy raven to fill a place of honor in my hoard of erudite smut (with permissions and blessings, of course).

This manuscript has been a joy for all involved, and in it you'll find lusty anonymous gropings, chem majors with erotic chemistry short-circuiting their logic functions, Peeping Toms and Peeping Thomasinas, boys who like boys who like girls, strong takes on rough men, sweetly rushed orgasms with celebrity crushes, and much more.

A college couple visit his family home in Vermont, and he gives his fiancée the ultimate Christmas present when he triple-teams her with his two identical brothers. A hacker finds himself in a predicament when he accidentally leaves his webcam on—and his female chat partner won't let him off the hook.

A female ghostwriter indulges a wealthy businessman, and he uses her for far more creative purposes than just ghostwriting—even loaning her out to his business associates. A woman becomes determined to find a dirty stranger to feel her up on the subway after watching a porn of public sex and groping—and she does.

The stories here were a delight to find, and we're excited to share them with you. We hope you enjoy this smart, arousing, sparkly treasure as much as we have.

Violet Blue
San Francisco

THE GHOSTWRITER

Valerie Alexander

A cold November drizzle streaked the windows of the conference room where I waited to see if my career was going to skyrocket. One of the most powerful men in business was six leather swivel chairs away from me, reviewing my portfolio on his laptop; the lights were off and the long table was surrounded by empty chairs that seemed filled with the ghosts of executives past.

Outside the conference room was a corridor of empty offices, an empty secretarial area and an elevator. We were alone up here on the forty-second floor.

I wished my back wasn't to the windows, so I could look out at the city and not at him. A financial genius, the media called him, famous for getting the best of every deal, a man who'd made the cover of *Forbes* and *Inc.* and all those other business magazines I'd written for. At fifty-eight he was stylishly handsome with thick salt-and-pepper hair and trendy glasses. But none of his photos had conveyed the dominant, slightly menacing charisma currently making my heart skip in erratic beats.

I waited for him to dismiss me. Send me back down to his company's marketing and PR departments who regularly hired me to ghostwrite articles for their executives. He won't pick me, I thought. He'll pick a famous ghostwriter with bestsellers for other industry titans under his or her belt.

Rain plopped on the glass.

"There will be the usual nondisclosure agreements," he said. "And you'll have to clear your calendar for the next few months." He lifted his green eyes from the laptop screen. "You would come to this conference room every day. Recording our sessions is fine, but I would need you here for at least three or four hours a day. The publication schedule is tight."

"That won't be a problem," I said. But I found it hard to believe he had three hours free a day. The executives I usually ghosted for could barely find twenty minutes to let me interview them.

"This won't be a typical business biography," he said. "More of a memoir. The company isn't hiring you, just to be clear. Your contract will be with me."

"I understand—" I had to cut myself off before calling him sir.

"You can call me Giles." He paused. "I've had an unconventional life outside the boardroom and part of that includes a deep immersion in BDSM. The principles of which aren't that different from business, as it happens. From your column, I gather you know something about that."

Now my heart began to bang hard in my chest. I wrote a column covering the local BDSM scene for an alternative weekly, but it was under a pen name entirely different from the name I used for ghostwriting. The thought of my corporate clients reading about my experiences with bondage, degradation and being a switch made my toes curl with embarrassment. But that was the thing about being a writer—you never knew who was reading.

He saw my expression. "A lot of people owe me favors," he said with a small smile. "Anyhow, I learned immensely useful lessons from BDSM and that connection will be spelled out. Nothing too graphic, but I need someone who won't be disturbed. Someone who will accept more...unorthodox methods of communication."

I nodded, suddenly aware of my visual presentation: my high heels on the carpet, my manicured hands gripping the armrests. My black suit and pearl earrings. "No disturbance here. I've been involved in some extreme edge play."

Then I stopped—I'd ghosted for enough executives to know that not one of them wanted to hear about the writer's private life. But his smile was amused; skeptical; at twenty-eight I was too young to grasp the extremity he'd seen, that smile let me know.

"You're the right person," he said.

We started two days later with Giles describing a brutal rite of passage when he joined the Marines. "Just hazing," he said. "Although hazing can serve a purpose, as you know."

I didn't know, but I nodded. He smiled grimly. "You've never been hazed."

"I—no."

Silence fell in the conference room. I waited for him to rise—fearful, throat tightening—and then felt disappointed when he said, "Well, I'm not going to haze you. So apparently you'll never know."

A charming smile. In just my few hours here, I'd already learned that he used that smile as a passport, getting himself into people's good graces and out of obligations.

"On to life after the military," he said. "I wanted to be impor-tant. No, that's wrong. I thought I already was important and I wanted that to be recognized."

I typed rapidly, never wanting the hypnotic spell of his voice to end. "You wanted validation?"

"I would never use that word," he said. "Don't use it." He glanced at the red light on my recorder. "I thought it was all about me and bulldozing my way in. Then I got a new boss, Rebecca. She taught me to stop thinking about myself and focus on the other person—the rival, the client, the customer. She showed me this by making me her dog and her slave. And I was a better man for it."

His smile twisted. "You have to realize how different everything was when I entered the workforce. Thirty-five years ago, people were just starting to talk about sexual harassment and most of us thought it was a joke."

"So you're saying you..."

"Slept my way to the top? Not exactly. More like I slept with a lot of men and women I met on the way up. And this woman changed my life. Masterfully."

He leaned back in the leather chair. "In finance, there is no stability. Interest rates rise and fall, the market plunges because of a CEO's remark, firms go bankrupt. So I learned early to stay agile, like a cat—and adapt as situations demanded."

He told me about making a faux pas at a client dinner one night and winding up in Rebecca's office with his pants down, bent over the desk, as she took her hairbrush to his bare ass again and again.

"I was humiliated and outraged and hard as iron. And I came at the end of it." He described how Rebecca shared him with the CEO of a petroleum company in a hotel suite, Giles stripping for the two of them and sliding his hard cock in the CEO's mouth.

"It's irresistible when someone knows what you want before you do," he said. "You wonder what else they know about you. They become your sexual oracle."

"Did she? Know what else you wanted, I mean?"

"Of course. The first time she tied me up, I thought I would explode. The absolute powerlessness and fighting her authority— then succumbing to my own need for that powerlessness, which is the true humiliation."

Recognition flooded my face in a warm blush. I tilted my head so that my hair covered my cheeks.

"I see that's how it is for you," he said.

I laughed nervously. My legs felt weak and my underwear was wet.

"I'll show you."

My stomach dropped as he rose and walked around the conference table. Against every professional code, he was going to take control of me and use me, just like I'd been hoping and dreading. I watched as he removed black nylon rope from his suit pockets and tied my wrists to the arms of the swivel chair.

"You look fetching like that," he said. "But overdressed."

He unbuttoned my pin-striped blouse and pushed the lace cups of my bra under my nipples. Then he gathered my loose brown hair behind my shoulders, to put me properly topless on display.

And then, to my immense disappointment, he walked back to his seat.

"I can't write like this," I said, hoping to be punished for complaining.

"You don't need to write," he said. "It's all being recorded. You need to listen."

I shifted restlessly against the ropes. But he only went into a story about his first major business deal before yawning abruptly and looking at his watch. "I have a meeting uptown."

Before untying me, he slid his hands over my breasts. "From now on, you'll be tied up while I dictate," he said, "and you'll transcribe the recording later."

He was almost doubling my workload with hours of tedious transcription. But I would have said yes to anything at that moment, and spending more time immersed in his world seemed a privilege anyhow. "If that's how you want it."

He untied me and I adjusted my clothes. I wondered why he wasn't fucking me right then, how he could stand to have an attractive and much younger woman tied up half-naked in his conference room.

"People are easier to manipulate before they come," he said as I packed up. "Not after. In business you want to make people fall in love with you, and then keep them short of satisfaction all the time for maximum pliability."

It had to take confidence, baldly stating his strategy. Then again, we both knew I wasn't going anywhere.

A cold, dreary December day. It was a routine now, taking the elevator up to the forty-second floor, so high I needed a special badge for access. Sometimes by the lobby fountain I ran into the marketing and PR directors I'd freelanced for and they'd ask how the book was going. I stayed vague. How could I tell them that their corporate god liked me to lay naked and spread-eagled on the table while he explained how to assess risk, seduce enemies and use people's vanity against them? He was a master in the dark arts of business domination and every day I learned his secrets. How to assassinate a rival's career. When to be invisible and when to be a star. How to identify companies and executives ripe for the plundering and make them think the plundering was their idea.

Today Giles was on the phone when I arrived. I strolled through the empty offices, looking at the unused mahogany furniture. How grand and stale it all was. The floor belonged to a lost era of commanding male executives and sexy secretaries and martinis in the office.

"Exploring?"

He leaned against the doorway in a charcoal-gray suit. No square glasses today. His green eyes were merciless.

"Just looking around. It's spooky up here. Why don't you have a secretary?"

"I do," he said. "She's on another floor. I like my privacy."

"Doesn't she mind?"

"She does what I tell her. Most people do."

He walked up to me and began unbuttoning my shirt. *Please touch me, please touch me,* I chanted silently.

But he didn't, not even when I stood naked in front of him. Instead he put a black leather collar around my throat and attached a leash to it. "Get on all fours."

He walked me like a dog down the long carpeted corridor to the conference room. Then he made me climb onto the table, still on all fours, and fastened my leash to a heavy ceiling-mounted projector.

If I'd felt on display other days, this was worse. I was an unwilling centerpiece, unable to move more than a few inches in any direction. And I was facing away from him, so that he got to look at my ass and cunt while I looked at a blank projection screen.

He took a seat behind me, switched on the recorder and began to talk. This time he relayed the story of a brilliant young man who worked for him and saved the day during some crisis, but Giles felt it better to withhold the credit. Instead he barely praised him, holding him at arm's length.

"You have to make people want to belong to you," he said. "Subordinates don't respect bosses who are too—enamored of them." He paused. "But I made a mistake in this case and I lost him."

He'd never talked about his mistakes before. I wondered if

it was easier for him to admit his errors without facing me.

His fingers moved across my pussy. With leisurely patience, he slid them inside me as he began describing a former rival. "The art of managing enemies is critical. This woman was a tiger in the equity capital markets area. I had to pretend to befriend her so I could study her. Find your enemies' power source and you've also found their Achilles' heel to take them down."

His fingers moved in and out of me.

"You took her down?" I managed to say.

"Discreetly. You never want credit for ruining someone—that's for amateurs. Do it right and everyone suspects enough to respect you, but the enemy doesn't know for sure if he should take revenge." His thumb moved over my clit.

I couldn't stand it. "Please," I begged. "Just fuck me. I can't concentrate."

His fingers withdrew. "Oh," he said. "You still think you have some control. I've failed in training you."

"No! You haven't failed! I'm sorry. I'll just—"

Giles undid his tie and came around the table, gagging me with it swiftly.

"Now," he said, settling back into his chair. His fingers pushed inside me again, agile and skilled. "Let's resume."

He didn't fuck me that day or the next and the following Monday he told me he was thinking of using another writer. "I just don't know that you're psychologically where I need you to be for this."

"I am," I said. "I swear."

He pulled me onto his lap and slipped his hand up my skirt. "I saw a rare insight in your column," he said. "An indication that you could appreciate a dark and complex education. That you could put everything I learned into words. But you haven't even learned basics like the importance of hiding your agenda."

In other words, by begging for his cock, I was handing him a tool to manipulate me. I said with all the dignity I could muster, "In the past, as a sub or a domme, I've never had to beg anyone to fuck me."

"Another lesson you haven't learned. Know who you're dealing with. Don't presume past strategies will work on present situations."

Giles pushed me off his lap and went to the window. "Your agenda should be satisfying me: writing the book I'm paying you to write," he said. "I'm going to Brazil this weekend. I'd like to pour out the bulk of this now and have you shape it into something while I'm gone."

"Okay," I said, though I didn't know what kind of turnaround time we were talking about.

"I want you to stay here in the office until then. Starting tomorrow, you'll sleep here and be at my beck and call, with no contact with the outside world."

Submitting to 24/7 play was not something I'd done before. But I wasn't going to refuse after he'd just told me how green I was.

The next day I returned with a packed bag that he immediately confiscated. I thought I would get it back when it came time to sleep, but I was wrong. Instead he made me crawl into one of the floor's lesser offices. A pillow from his office sofa adorned the floor; he chained my ankle to the credenza, with just enough leeway to reach the private office bathroom and the several bottles of water on the desk. A desk phone assured me help was only a call away, but I also understood that to call for help in anything less than an emergency would end our arrangement immediately.

Then Giles pulled out a chastity belt. A very sophisticated one, designed for long-term use.

"No," I said immediately. My hands and vibrators were the only relief I'd had these last few weeks from the throbbing, soaking fever he worked me into every day. There was no way I could go the rest of the week without being able to touch myself.

"No?" His brows lifted.

After a moment I forced out, "Yes." And I hated him a little as he locked my pussy under his control.

My first night alone was spooky. His stories echoed in my mind, the mentors and celebrities he'd seduced, the rivals who'd knelt before him, his longstanding love for a colleague who had whipped him until he wept. The thought of him in tears or sternly wielding a crop or coming on his boss's face made me groan. I imagined the day he might be chained and naked before me, my slave to fuck and devour as long as I wanted. And all the while my cunt throbbed hopelessly in the chastity belt.

My mother and friends thought I was on a business trip somewhere without cell phone coverage. Without Internet access, television or my phone, I felt bereft. But each morning I woke to the glorious sound of the elevator opening down the hall—and there was my Master, his wry smile the most beautiful sight of my life.

"Come on," he said that Friday, snapping on my leash and walking me down the carpeted hallway to his office.

I'd been naked for enough days that clothes seemed like a distant memory. He unlocked my chastity belt and handed me breakfast from the company cafeteria, to eat with my fingers. Then it was time to shower in front of him. I had no privacy, no chance to make myself come, but I had no chance of seducing him either. As I soaped myself up in his office bathroom shower as sexily as I could, he only looked bored.

"I'll decide when I'm going to fuck you and all the sex tricks in the world won't sway me until then."

I scowled and he pulled me abruptly out of the shower, still wet and sudsy, to sprawl over his lap. I gasped, more from shock, as his hand came down hard on my ass.

"That expression of yours is incredibly ungrateful, considering the opportunity I'm giving you," he said, spanking me again and again. This wasn't the measured punishment he normally dealt out. This was passionate, severe, spontaneous. "Do you know how many people would like to be here, learning from me? How many emails I get every day from politicians, leaders at the top of their field, who beg for just fifteen minutes of my time?"

I opened my legs as wide as I could. He yanked me backward and began slapping my pussy, the first contact with my clit in days. I moaned and pushed myself against his hand, my wet skin swollen and sensitive. His fingers drove inside me, two or three of them, fucking me roughly while the slaps continued to rain down on my clit.

And then he stopped. He pushed me onto the floor.

"See, this is how I know you're not ready. Because a good sub would put my needs over her own."

He was flustered. He had lost control, finally, and given in to what I knew now was a genuine hunger to punish and fuck me.

"I do put your needs first. I am going to write you the best book ever—"

"You can't write the book I want you to write until you understand leadership and submission. How I got where I am. How I inspired some of the most powerful people in the world to obey me."

"I'm sorry—"

"You're still not getting it."

He leashed me and walked me down to the conference room,

ordering me to sit on the floor while he dictated. His voice was curt and I knew he was truly distracted when our Thai lunch arrived and he allowed me to eat it with the plastic fork provided.

In late afternoon he positioned me before the windows with my hands cuffed overhead and my feet locked into a spreader bar.

"I have a meeting," he said. "I'll be back."

I watched night rise in the city, the lonely brilliance of Christmas in New York.

What he wanted from me was so difficult. He didn't want a younger woman on her knees—he could have had that the first week. And he didn't just want me to write the elegant business prose I'd delivered for so many of his kind. He wanted my transformation. He wanted to blow my sexual and professional limitations open and push me through an accelerated gauntlet of the mind-fucking he'd mastered over three decades in business.

All writers know that feedback from the right person is a gift. Criticism can be a road map to brilliance when a brilliant person is delivering it. His investment in my development could be the ultimate compliment, if I truly was his protégé. But more likely I was just another underling being seduced into doing his bidding. He was giving me the psychological keys to the castle only so I could reproduce that castle in print. At least that had been my thinking until today.

I heard the distant hum of the elevator doors opening on the floor. My stomach lurched.

The conference room door opened. I went stiff as I heard two people enter. Unsuccessfully I tried to look over my shoulder but I was bound too tightly.

Footsteps of a third person, followed by the snapping on of lights.

"There she is," Giles said. "If she's not to your taste, there's a house two blocks away that has some quality girls."

So I was to be fucked at last, but by two strangers—not by his unattainable cock. I swallowed nervously as a man approached the window to look at my face. He was in his late thirties and in a crisp blue button-down shirt.

"I heard you're desperate for cock," he said in a British accent. "I heard you've been pestering Giles for weeks, and he's had about enough of it."

This was a new level of humiliation. I stared out the window, refusing to react.

The Brit spanked me, hard. Then he slid two fingers inside me and did it again, so hard it pushed my body forward and his fingers farther up my pussy. It felt enough like getting fucked that I couldn't help whimpering. He laughed and began spanking me again and again until his fingers were thrusting in and out of me.

"Enough," said a strange male voice behind me. "Get her on the table."

The spanking stopped. With a jingle of keys, the Brit unlocked my ankles and wrists and I fell onto the conference-room carpet, my limbs shaking after so many hours in bondage.

I looked around for Giles but the other man picked me up immediately and arranged me on the table. He was in his forties, with a lean, stern face that barely changed as he pushed inside me without a word. He rode me with an impersonal rhythmic pumping that said I could be any girl at all, his tie dangling in my face. But he did something unexpected; he pulled out, came in his cupped hand and then smeared his come all over my face. "There," he said. "Now you look like the whore you are."

I stared at him in shock and wonder, but the Brit was already pushing me over one of the swivel chairs. My stomach came up against the cool leather, my ass in the air, and I knew what was going to happen even before he wet his fingers inside me and wiped them around my anus.

He shoved himself in my ass as thoughtlessly as the other one had taken me. It was degradation heaven, a stranger pounding my bottom while another stranger who'd just called me a whore looked on with boredom and contempt. I closed my eyes and wished desperately Giles would step up next, would take off his suit with that measured, graceful menace and grip my neck and fuck me deeper and harder than any man had before. Just thinking of it made my body go wet and hot like my nerves were being electrified and I screamed as an orgasm shook my entire body. The man responded by grabbing my hair and pulling me backward.

"You filthy slut," he said and slapped my breasts, making my orgasm go on and on like a thunderous bell that wouldn't stop ringing. I didn't even realize he had come until he dropped me on the carpet.

"Well," said Giles. "Shall we? We were expected for drinks an hour ago."

I looked up plaintively from the floor. Giles wouldn't look at me; I knew then I really had gotten under his skin. The other men took me to my office, locking me to the desk with a bag full of takeout Italian next to me.

If I hadn't been so exhausted and hungry, I would have wept. Instead I wolfed down the linguine and soup and fell asleep.

I awoke at the usual hour, grayish light creeping around the office venetian blinds. Only something was different: I was curled up in a ball. At some point in the night I had been unlocked. And there was a pile on the desk—my bag of clothes and my purse.

I grabbed my phone. There were texts from friends and my mom saying they hoped my business trip was going well. But it was the text from Giles I read first.

On my way to São Paulo. I'll be back after the holidays. Be prepared to show me what you've done.

I cried once I got back to my apartment, tears of release and a strange joy I didn't quite understand. I wasn't the person who'd written my old columns on BDSM. I was becoming someone else. That weekend I wrote for hours, pouring out notes, ideas and outlines. I knew this was how Giles operated, manipulating everyone into serving his interests, making me so desperate for his approval that I would sacrifice anything to write a beautiful book with his name on it. But I couldn't resent his mastery because one day it would be my mastery too.

Twelve days later, a text arrived, instructing me to watch the news. And there was his headshot as the anchor reported another company merger and more shockingly, his retirement. A tell-all biography could be expected next year, a memoir that reportedly already had many in the business world nervous.

My phone rang. "It's real now. I hope you're ready for what's ahead," Giles said.

"I'm ready for anything."

He laughed. "That only proves you have no idea what I'm capable of."

I bit back the temptation to beg for details or try to beguile him or ask when he was returning. Instead I said, "The book is coming along well."

I could hear his smile over the phone. "I knew I could expect great things from you."

ROXANNE

Tamsin Flowers

The Geeks Shall Inherit the Earth. That's what they say. It's everybody's favorite T-shirt slogan. Hell, I even have that shirt myself somewhere at the back of my closet. My mom gave it to me as a gesture of affection but believe me, I've never worn it. I've already got the geek thing going—glasses, flat chest, high scores in science classes—without having to advertise the fact. Oh, and did I mention my nose? The nose I was born with that precedes me wherever I go by several seconds? That little kids shelter under to get out of the rain? No, that shirt is redundant as far as I'm concerned.

I'm a geek girl. I accept who I am. I hang out with other geek girls and I never talk to boys. And, on the whole, I'm happy with my life. Or I was.

Until I got sat next to Roxanne in Physics 360.

Roxanne is a goddess. Tall, slim, athletic, beautiful, with long blonde hair—you know, all the attributes that go with the word. And whip smart too, always top of the class. So if you thought this was going to be one of those stories in which the geek earns the undying gratitude of the beauty by helping her with her senior term paper, then, no, you got it wrong. She made better grades than I did. And I was desperately in love with her.

"Syra, isn't it?" she said, as she brought her books over to my bench.

I nodded, dumbfounded by the twist of fate that had launched her in my direction. She'd never spoken to me before. She sat down next to me and spread out her stuff, shaking her head.

"It's so good to sit next to you," she said. My heart fluttered a little. "At least you won't be hitting on me for my homework or trying to copy stuff over my shoulder."

Of course. I'd forgotten for a moment that I was the geek. But she hadn't.

I spluttered and went bright red, like I always do at the worst times. Then class started and we got down to business. Sitting next to each other made us lab partners and we settled quickly into a routine—conducting the experiments, writing our reports, hitting straight A's. Occasionally Roxanne would try to engage me in conversation and I slowly started to come out of my shell. As long as we were talking about science. Of course, outside class she still had to ignore me. She had her own credibility to worry about and she wouldn't maintain queen-bee status if she was seen talking to me. I didn't mind.

What I did mind, though, was when she started going on about Christian Neville. He was new—transferred from some college out East. He was on the football team. His dad had been a pro footballer. He was astoundingly good-looking, according to Roxanne. His body…I forget the rest. I sort of tuned out when she started talking about him. She had it bad.

"I think I'm in love," she announced one Tuesday morning as we were investigating stellar time scales. My heart fluttered a little at her words. But then: "I'm in love with Christian."

Of course. I'd forgotten for a moment I was the girl with the out-of-proportion nose. But she hadn't.

It came as a body blow when I was allocated the seat next to Christian Neville in Physics 380. I could see from his face when he saw me coming, preceded by my proboscis, that it was a blow to him too. We didn't chat and Physics 380 wasn't collaborative. But he did attempt collaboration by looking over my shoulder while I made the necessary calculations for our class assignments. I took to wrapping my other arm around my paper to stop him from seeing. I could sense his frustration at this by the way he slammed his pen down on the bench.

"Come on, Syra, play fair," he whined. "You know I can do all this stuff, but it'll just take me till after class finishes and I've got to get to training."

He tried flashing his megawatt smile, but he obviously hadn't realized I wasn't into guys.

"Please," he pouted. "Or…"

"Or what?" I said, looking up at him.

"Jeez, watch out with the nose, would you? Nearly had my eye out."

"Bigger than your dick, is it?"

He pulled a face.

"God knows what she sees in you," I muttered to myself as I finished off my calculus.

"What? Who?"

I ignored him.

"Syra, who are you talking about?" he said, fixing me with pleading, puppy-dog eyes. "Tell me it's Roxanne. Is it? Is it?"

Even though I despised him, I had to admit there was a boyish charm about Christian Neville that could soften the hardest of hearts, and mine certainly wasn't that.

"You like her?" I said, forgetting the nose jibe. I'd heard it all before.

"Like her? That's my future ex-wife you're talking about."

"So ask her out."

Christian went red as cherry-pie filling and I stared at him.

He nodded. "Yeah, this is what happens every time I try to talk to her."

I could relate to that.

"So text her," I said. Yes. I am that expert at giving dating advice to lovelorn jocks and broken-hearted he-men.

"You think?" Christian's teeth were so goddamn white.

He held out his cell phone and I took it—I don't know why. And that's how it started. I typed in a text.

Want 2 compare magnetic attraction coefficients Thurs night?
I showed him.

"Seriously? I don't even know what that means."

"She will."

"How well d'you know her?"

"I sit next to her in Physics 360."

That seemed to satisfy him. He hit SEND and ten minutes later she replied.

Horizontal or vertical?
He showed me her text, his chest heaving with excitement.

Up 2 you, I texted back.

CU Thurs.

"Fuck me, Syra, you did it," he said loud enough to earn us a harsh look from the professor.

He did a little wiggle with his arms. "Gonna get laid. Gonna get laid."

That stuck in my craw some and I should have called a halt right then, but this was a love story and I was hooked.

"Say, send her another," he said, giving me the cell.

I thought about what I'd like to do with Roxanne.
How do u feel about us & spintroncis?
I passed the cell back to him.
"Oh boy," said Christian, with a low whistle.
I could actually see he had a hard-on. Her reply pinged in.
I held out my hand for the phone and he passed it over. Text
sex—sexting—it's what our generation is all about, they'd have
you believe. I was sexting with Roxanne. She thought she was
sexting with Christian. And, of course, when it got to exchanging
pictures on Snapchat, she was. But I got my cheap thrill and
Christian got his date.

Maybe you don't have an opinion on whether the U.K. version
of "Being Human" is better than the U.S. one. That's okay. But
plenty of people do and I was following a discussion board on
that very topic when Christian's text came in.
Help…what do I say?
I looked at my watch. He was out for dinner with Roxanne if
things had gone according to plan. Oh yes, he'd stunned her with
his erudite texting and now he needed to be witty and seductive in person. I dragged myself away from a thread debating
whether George was more convincingly lupine than Josh. There
was a real human in need of my dating prowess.
I replied to his text.
*Talk physics. Her term paper = magnetic field fusion. U want
2 fuse ur magnetic fields…*
This could go badly wrong, I thought as I pressed SEND. It
happens I was right. Without wanting to bore you with more
science—physicists can apply in writing for the full tran-
script—I led Christian through a series of increasingly risqué
innuendos. We covered Planck energy, nanobot reproduction,
gray goo scenarios and ramjet fusion in a series of increasingly

frenzied text exchanges. God, to have been a fly in the soup at that table!

There was a lull in the conversation.

How does she not realize ur texting under the table?

Holding her hostage with my blue eyes.

It's true—they were a remarkable shade of blue.

Leaving now. Thanks 4 help.

U owe me.

Ur right. Coming round 2 deliver.

What? That didn't read right.

There was a knock on my door. WTF? It was past eleven and I don't have the sort of friends who just drop by. Christian should have been on his way back to Roxanne's, so this couldn't be him. Could it?

I put down my phone and padded to the door just as my caller knocked for a second time.

"What are you doing here?" I said, pulling the door open and expecting to find Christian outside.

But it wasn't him.

Roxanne held Christian's cell up to my face. I read the screen.

I want to explore your carbon nanotubes.

I wrote those words. He must have said them.

Roxanne pushed through the door and backed me up against the wall. Her face was flushed and she was close enough for me to smell alcohol on her breath. I wondered how large my nose looked at such close range.

"You wrote every single word of it, didn't you?" she said.

I nodded.

"And you meant it?" Her tone softened.

I nodded again. I couldn't have articulated at that moment if my life depended on it.

Her kiss was a savage surprise. Her mouth crushed against mine, slamming my head back against the wall, giving me two reasons for seeing stars. No one had ever kissed me like this before—tongue thrusting into my mouth, pushing against mine, slipping past it to explore. I felt heat rising from the furnace between my legs and I kissed her back in a way I'd never kissed anyone before. Our noses clashed and she drew back, laughing.

"What about Christian?" I asked.

"It was so obvious it wasn't him," she said. "I could tell someone was putting words in his mouth, and I could see him texting in his lap."

"Where is he now?"

"I left him paying the bill. He was very red in the face and trying to disguise a huge hard-on with his serviette."

Her hand strayed to the zipper of my hoodie and started slowly drawing it down.

"I took his phone. I had to see who it was."

"I thought you had feelings for him."

She pushed my hoodie back over my shoulders as we staggered through to the living room.

"They evaporated as soon as he went off script."

She yanked up my T-shirt and pulled it roughly over my head.

"As soon as I realized it was you, there was only one thing I could think of."

I knew what it was. There are certain very specific uses for a big nose that you probably only appreciate when you've gone out with someone thus blessed.

I directed her back onto the settee and knelt on the floor in front of her. She leaned forward and sucked one of my breasts into her mouth. My nipple pebbled at the touch of her tongue, and I almost cried with relief. I pushed her dress up her thighs until it rucked around her hips while her fingers worked to make my other nipple as hard.

"You know why I'm here." Her lips moved against the dark, puckered skin of my areola. I wished she'd keep talking. But then I wished more that she'd carry on doing what she was doing with her tongue.

I hooked my fingers into the top of her black-lace panties and drew them down. These were the panties she'd put on for her date with Christian. Now I was taking them off. They glided down her long, slim legs but she had to let go of my breasts as I tangled with the panties over the heels of her stilettos.

"Here, let me," she said.

She leaned forward to undo the shoe buckles at the side of her ankles and I took advantage of her position to slide a hand into the top her dress. Her chest was tightly encased in smooth satin, the sort of sexy slip of a bra that would never grace my own lingerie drawer. I pushed one cup aside and yanked her breast free of it. She gasped and even though her shoes and panties were free, she remained where she was to let me play for a minute.

"Now," she said, leaning back on the couch and spreading her legs apart.

The smell of her musk caught at the back of my throat as I leaned in. If being a physicist didn't prevent me from believing in God, I would have thought I'd died and gone to heaven. I rested my forearms on her thighs, pressing out to keep her spread wide. She was clean shaven and in the dying light of the day the dark crevice at the top of her legs glistened. She was wet and I licked my lips in anticipation.

The first taste of woman is always a revelation, just like the first kiss. She tasted good, sweet and unique, and I instantly knew I was going to want more of this. I swept the line where her lips met with my tongue. I heard her sharp intake of breath above me and felt her hips pushing into the couch, her legs stretching wider. I brought my tongue down in the opposite direction and let the tip of my nose press against her soft flesh. She moaned. I used a finger to ease her lips apart, allowing a deluge of warm juices to escape. I inserted my finger farther, delighting in the velvety softness of the cavern I was exploring. Deep in my pelvis, I ached to feel her touch in return. My muscles clenched as I ground my hips back against my heels.

I pulled my finger out, spreading her lips open with my hand. I used my tongue to caress and massage her wet folds, darting in and out, playing hide-and-seek with the tip of my nose, sticking my tongue out as far as I could and pushing it up inside her. At the same time I reached 'round to the back of her hips and pulled her forward onto the edge of the couch. My face was buried in a place that up until now had only existed in my imagination. But this was one-hundred-percent real and her hips flexed against me, demanding more.

My fingers dug into the soft flesh of her buttocks and she grunted. I fucked her with my tongue, in and out, rubbing my nose into the soft flesh above. When she pushed up against me, I slipped my tongue out and let it drop farther. She gasped as I made a tentative foray toward the tight pucker of her ass. Sweet, soft flicks with my tongue—and each time I touched against it, I could feel her muscles tighten sharply, then gradually relax. I pressed my nose into her cunt and pushed against her resistant ass with my mouth. It was easy to slide a finger down her crack to do the hard work and in a few moments she opened up to me.

I finger-fucked her ass until she couldn't keep still on the couch and she put a hand down to stop me. I raised my eyes and her beauty shocked me anew, like I'd forgotten who I'd gone down on. Or at least I couldn't believe who it was.

"Let me taste you," she said.

"Of course." My voice was hoarse.

I stood up and pulled off my yoga pants as if they were on fire, almost tripping in my enthusiasm. My barely there G-string followed and I was ready for her. All right, more than ready. I'd been wet since our first kiss in the hall and clenching since I'd taken in the first deep breath of her musky scent. She swung her legs up onto the couch and lay back with her head on one armrest. I bent to kiss her but she pointed down toward the other end.

Classic sixty-nine with Roxanne. This was my favorite dream—and probably Christian's as well—made flesh. I faced away from her and straddled her now-naked body, bending forward and shuffling back until I reached the ideal position. She bent her knees up and let her tawny legs fall wide. We hit each other at the same moment, causing muffled gasps and a suppressed giggle.

"Beautiful," she whispered against my quivering folds.

It's not a word I've had directed at me very often, so I sucked her clit into my mouth for the gentlest of kisses. She started exploring me with her fingers and her tongue at the same time, opening me up like she was unwrapping a gift, bussing me with her lips, blowing sweet sighs on hot flesh. My back arched as I pushed against her. What she was doing to me was distracting me from what I was doing to her. And what I was doing to her was distracting me from what she was doing to me. But somehow the twin pleasures collided at my center.

My tongue dipped into her for a taste of nectar and then I drew it up between swollen lips to find her clit. It was distended, and I sucked it greedily into my mouth. At the same time I pushed down with my nose, deep into her cleft, pulling on her clit with my teeth as I did.

She swirled her tongue in circles around mine. She had two fingers high inside me, pressing and caressing the soft spot in perfect time with the movement of her mouth. I moaned and bit down harder. She yelped and then sucked. She added a third finger, plunging in and out of me, flicking me with her tongue in a way that sent a volley of shock waves up my spine and out along my neural paths.

My face was so far into her I could hardly breathe, but I didn't care. I was drinking her instead, and it was better than oxygen. Pulses of pleasure fired through me—an electrifying climax that made my head spin and left me reeling. The attachment of my mouth to her clit was all that anchored me and I felt her muscles clench hard as her own orgasm exploded through her.

I slumped sideways against the back of the couch, gasping for air. My body was wet with sweat and still trembling. She pulled me 'round clumsily to lie against her, face-to-face.

"Ramjet fusion?" she said.

"Nuh-uh," I said. "Spintronics. Ramjet fusion involves a strap-on."

She nodded. "Makes sense."

I kissed her nearest nipple.

"It's a pity we have Christian's cell phone here," she said.

"Why?"

"I think he might have appreciated a Snapchat of this!"

CLICK-CLICK-CLICK

Annabeth Leong

I didn't know if Ron had made it to town yet, but I could feel his eyes on me anyway, uncovering the sexiest version of me.

I spent the first day in Burlington wandering around, shopping for clothes or camping gear or whatever was being sold in stores with nice, unobstructed windows. My movements became languid, unhurried and artful. I lost my fear of taking up space. Getting a jacket down from a rack wasn't just about reaching for a coat hanger and shrugging cloth away. Instead, I discovered the sensual joy of letting my purse slip down my leg to rest atop my upturned foot, pressing my breasts forward as I worked my shoulders back to free myself of my current denim, then stretching my bared arms wide as I spread out new leather and breathed in its scent.

All day long, I imagined the click-click-click camera sound effect that gets played in movies when someone photographs a character from afar, and accompanied it with visions of a telephoto lens and Ron at the other side, manipulating the focus with one big hand and timing his exhales so as not to jog the device.

My voyeur and I had never met in person, but he was the one who came to mind whenever someone asked if I had a boyfriend. Our arrangement had lasted five years by then. Every couple of months I traveled for a weekend to a town I didn't know and gave Ron hints about where I'd be. He always sent me the pictures afterward, and it made me feel like a celebrity to sit down at my kitchen table at home and deal out the glossy eight-by-ten prints he'd made of me, some in color and some in black-and-white. He usually caught some shots of me getting undressed before bed, sliding my panties down my thighs, but others he grabbed while I was out doing seemingly ordinary things, crowning me with unexpected sexiness. The pictures were erotic but generally not explicit, and more than once I'd caught myself wondering how my pussy would appear under his lens.

I knew that paparazzi often make celebrities miserable, but Ron and I inhabited a soft-focus fantasy version of that life, not the real thing, and god it made me hot.

Ron was at least a friend, but it was also easy to fantasize that I was a little in love with him. The longer we played the game, the more I felt it changing me, and even when I knew Ron wasn't there to see, I often caught myself standing with a certain thrust of the hip or idly sliding the hem of my dress a few dangerous inches upward.

By the time the Burlington trip rolled around, I was looking for a way to take things up a notch with Ron. As I tried on clothes and flirted with Ron's possibly present camera, I decided to skip the usual text messages we shared during our weekend vacations and make his paparazzi role feel more authentic.

Shutting off my phone, I picked up a bottle of red wine on the way back to my cabin in the woods outside of town and, once there, did my best impression of believing myself to be absolutely alone. Out on the back porch with a citronella candle and a book, I sipped a glass and pondered my next move.

The wine heated my skin, and I pulled off my light denim jacket, then kicked off my shoes, and finally used my big toes to peel away my socks. I flexed and pointed my bare feet, admiring my new pedicure and the shapeliness of my arches. Ron had proven partial to unexpected aspects of my anatomy, awakening me to the erotic potential of the curve of my earlobe and the profile of my naked calves. I ran a finger down my leg, my nerves awakening to the beautiful lines that Ron had revealed.

I allowed my hand to travel, and it seemed as if I was discovering myself for the first time. Knees. Thighs. Hips. Ribs.

Ron had photographed me topless a few times, and my pussy pulsed at the memory of the grainy black-and-white shots. They had made me feel like a foreign film star from a bygone era. My breasts had seemed so abundant, my nipples expressive, my unconcerned features impossibly sensual.

I wanted to bare myself right there on the porch, sunbathing with the casual entitlement of the rich and famous. After all that time, though, I wasn't sure exactly what Ron liked. Would he enjoy seeing me display myself deliberately, or would he read the act as tasteless and too obvious?

I toyed with my shirt as I considered, and with every breath I became more aware of my cunt. I pressed my thighs together for the pleasure of the tension, and gave in to a rhythmic set of squeezes.

The shivers running through my pelvis were just the sort of open secret I had enjoyed while downtown thinking of Ron. My hand hovered between the hem of my shirt and the waistline of my pants, but it didn't stray anywhere overtly sexual. I was sure, however, that my face betrayed what I was feeling. I could imagine the way a picture of me might look. Lips swollen with desire, eyelids half-lowered to partially conceal gathering sexual heat, nostrils flared, head flung back to an angle that revealed the length of my neck.

I adjusted the angle of my head to match my vision and closed my fingers around the top button of my fly. Instead of stripping on the porch, I teased myself and possibly Ron. A subtle tug on the button made the reinforced denim of my fly rub my clit through my panties. I yanked a little harder, until my outer labia parted around the cloth.

Reaching up to scratch the back of my neck, I pulled my bra strap along the way and closed my eyes to absorb the sensation of my breasts shifting and my nipples sliding along the insides of the silky cups that held them.

My hips rolled up of their own accord. I'd gotten myself almost hot enough to come. If Ron was watching, maybe he was wondering if I was going to actually touch myself. I wanted to, but a better idea interrupted my fingers before they could travel to my clit. A naughtier one.

With the speed of decision, I sat up and examined the wineglass. I hadn't made much progress with its contents, and I was certainly sober enough to drive. I kicked aside my jacket and socks, opting instead to go out with more skin showing and wearing a sexy pair of heels I grabbed out of my luggage.

I preferred friends with benefits as sex partners, or at the very least online hookups with a decent amount of email and text messages first. Meeting a stranger cold was trickier—there was always the question of whether I would see anyone I liked, or if I'd say the right things. Maybe I should have worried about safety, but the idea of Ron watching made me feel as if I wasn't doing this alone.

Swinging into the bar, I felt like a character in a movie. Gravel crunched beneath my pumps, my hips swayed and I turned heads as I swept into the room and headed for the bartender. I ordered a whiskey shot, not because I normally drink hard liquor but because the person I was pretending to be would.

In seconds, men buzzed around me. Maybe it would have happened regardless of what I'd been feeling—Ron's pictures had been forcing me to recognize my own loveliness—but I believed the men were attracted to the sexiness oozing out of me, the show that I was still putting on for Ron.

Having my pick of men made me feel decadent, as if I'd gone shopping at a high-end store. I wanted someone interestingly photogenic. Not the generic Adonis common to underwear commercials, but the sort of person whose looks might be ugly and might be beautiful.

It didn't take long to spot him. The man bore acne scars on his cheeks and the uneasy squint of someone only recently acquainted with contact lenses. But there was also a grace to his hands and a poetic something about his lips. He was dressed as if he'd just gotten off work at a bank, but he'd stretched his earlobes around large, black, wooden discs. His skin looked warm and golden.

I glanced toward him more than once, and the shape of his face seemed to change at each new angle. In profile, his high, sharp cheekbones stood out. Straight on, I noticed roundness at his jaw that softened his appearance. Despite the abundance of hipsters in Burlington, he was clean shaven. He caught me looking, and the side of his mouth curled up into a smile that would have been arrogant if he hadn't immediately ducked his head to study his hands with more interest than they warranted.

I grinned to myself and carried my whiskey over to him, getting a little thrill from the obvious disappointment of the men I left behind to do so. His name was Jonas. I talked to him for a while, mostly because I sensed that he needed to be set at ease.

He was interested, though, and clearly looking for company, so eventually I let my toe tease the side of his calf. His eyes widened, and the wonder in his expression gave me a rush of power. His coarse black hair tickled my lips as I leaned in close to whisper in his ear. "I'm not in town for long," I told him, "but I'm here tonight…"

I didn't have to say much else. Everyone wants to be desired. I told him that I liked the way he smelled, and then I admitted that I wanted to see him naked. I told him that the moment I saw him, I wondered what his fingers would feel like inside my pussy.

At that, he gripped my wrist. "Can I take you somewhere? You can find out."

I smiled and pressed my breast against his arm. "I've got a cabin."

He chatted nervously on the drive. I could tell he wasn't used to being picked up by a woman, and wasn't used to riding in the passenger seat. The wheels turning in his head were practically visible. I knew he'd seize any chance to take control of the way this night was going, but as long as he let me get us to the spot I had in mind, I was down for whatever he wanted.

My car bounced along the dirt road that led to my cabin. Jonas cleared his throat. "Do you just…do this? Like, often?"

I shot him a sideways look. I hoped he wasn't the type of man who needs a woman to pretend it's been a while. "If I do?"

He shrugged. "If you do, then I'll assume you, um, know what you're doing."

I felt my expression soften. I took one hand off the steering wheel to touch his thigh. "I want us both to have fun tonight. I'm not going to make you play guessing games. I'll tell you what I want to do, and you should do the same for me."

Jonas blinked, then grinned. "It's too bad you're not in town for long. I think I could get used to you."

I told him the truth. "Sometimes, it's more fun this way." There was, after all, a reason that Ron had been my most regular liaison for the past several years. I loved the thrill of pursuit and the first blush of discovery. Fighting over the covers—not so much.

I parked beside my cabin and pretended to stretch my neck. Really, I was checking for any hint of Ron's presence. The trees around my little wooden structure were dark and silent, but I thought I could feel him there nonetheless.

Turning back to Jonas, I started us off with a long kiss, leaning over the parking brake, stabilizing myself with one hand on his thigh and the other on his chest. I took control, my lips on the outside, my tongue pressing into his mouth. When I pulled back, he was breathless, and I rested my forehead against his to let him recover.

"Now you," I whispered.

He came at me slowly, pressing a series of kisses along my jaw, lingering at the corners of my lips. His fingers brushed my cheek, the gesture romantic, and I inhaled the clean spice of his aftershave as he took my mouth. I was getting impatient, sliding my hands under his shirt, but Jonas stopped me, catching my wrists and pushing my arms back toward my sides. Being forced to slow down stoked my desire more firmly. I had time to notice the way his tongue stroked mine, the heat of his fingers, the proximity of his teeth.

My thoughts went to Ron again. Could his lens capture my body's growing need? What would it reveal about the way Jonas touched me?

My lover released my mouth, and I saw my own lust reflected in his dark eyes. Under the light and shadow coming off my cabin's door light, Jonas was breathtaking, the in-between quality that had attracted me at the bar transforming him into a work of art.

"Let's get out of the car," he said.

"Do you need anything?" I asked, as I worked the key in the front door. "A drink?"

"You know what I need," he growled into my ear. Jonas tugged me toward the bedroom, but I pulled him to the back porch.

"I want to be outside," I told him. My throat tightened, and I revealed more than I'd intended. "I want to do it where we could be seen."

As soon as the words were out, I bit my lip, worried that I'd put him off, but Jonas gripped my hand tightly and led me to the edge of the porch. He settled my body against the railing, facing the trees, and stepped in close behind me to let me feel the hard length of his cock. "You should have told me earlier, baby. I would have done you in the parking lot behind the bar."

He dipped his mouth to my neck while he eased my shirt open.

"Would you have enjoyed that? Getting fucked against the trunk of your car?" He stuttered a little on the dirty talk, but I liked that Jonas was warming up for me.

I shivered and shook my head, managing a laugh through my arousal. "I want the risk, but I don't want to have to hurry."

"Oh. You want to stay out here all night."

Leaning my head back against Jonas's chest, I smiled for Ron. "All night. What do you want?"

"I want to put my fingers inside you."

Jonas lifted my breasts out of my bra, and I undid my pants so he could get his wish. Kicking off my heels and stepping out of my jeans, I guided one of his hands to my pussy.

The day had been warm, but the night air was cool on my bare legs. I thought of that camera click as Jonas cupped my cunt in his palm, and then began to probe my labia through my panties.

I was wet enough to moisten the fabric as it slid between my lips. Jonas sucked air in through his teeth as he slipped a finger under the elastic and found his way to my entrance. "You're dripping."

"I know." I couldn't stop thinking about how I looked from the woods. Arching my back to give him better access to my pussy, I bent forward so that my breasts spilled over the porch railing. My hair fell across my face, and I imagined the sense of mystery that could bring to a picture, my expression hidden except for the outer curve of my smile.

Jonas pushed my panties down to my knees. He traced a circle around my entrance with one fingertip, and my knees quivered. I liked that he took his time playing in the folds rather than just plunging in. A second finger joined the first, teasing me open, stretching me experimentally. With his other hand, he toyed with my clit, manipulating the hood, brushing lightly over the exposed bundle of nerves, rubbing the sides of the shaft.

"How do my fingers feel?"

"Amazing."

"Was it just my fingers you wanted?" He bumped his erection against my ass, and I grinned over my shoulder and pretended to consider.

"You've got a good point," I said finally. "I think I might like your tongue as well."

Jonas chuckled. "Greedy."

But he got to his knees.

I turned around and drew his head to my crotch. If I'd had a camera, I'd have been taking pictures myself. I adored his shapes and lines. His cheekbones seemed alien in the half-light, and moisture glittered on the tip of his tongue when he pressed it toward me. He didn't have enough hair to grip, so I petted the back of his head once and then tucked my hands behind me so as not to obstruct my view.

His tongue felt good, don't get me wrong. Jonas had an excellent sense of pacing. He was patient and precise. What was really getting me off, however, was thinking about the shots Ron could be taking. Would he like it from behind, where it might not even be clear that I was getting head? I could imagine the sexy subtlety in the angle of my spine, the way my fingers knotted together, the bend of my neck as I looked down at Jonas. Or would Ron prefer a side angle, one that showed Jonas's lips against my mound and the panties that had slipped farther down my legs to curl around my ankles? What angles could he capture with that miracle camera of his? Was it possible for him to get under the porch and take shots upward through the slats? Could he manage a picture of my pussy oozing juices onto Jonas's chin? Could he capture the spread of my legs?

I threw my head back and came against Jonas's mouth, dreaming all the while of Ron photographing my cunt in extreme close-up. Its spasms of pleasure felt all the more emphatic and intoxicating as I envisioned them in black-and-white, printed on high-quality matte paper.

Jonas slipped a finger inside me as I came, and it deepened my pleasure to clench around him. "You've got quite a grip," he murmured after I wound down.

I raised an eyebrow. "You'll feel it more if you put in something bigger."

"So I get to use that condom in my wallet after all."

"Very much so. And maybe even a few of the condoms in mine. If you're actually up for staying out here all night."

"You're going to have to drag me off this porch in the morning."

I bent over to kiss him, taking a moment to lick around his lips and taste my own juices. "What's your favorite position?"

"I want you to ride me."

I grinned. I could already see it. Breasts bouncing, arms flailing, thighs flexing. Animalistic lust on my face. His cock kissing my outer lips and then pushing its way through and inside as I lowered myself onto him. I shivered at the thought of how all that would look.

Nudging Jonas with a toe, I peeled away the rest of my clothes. "Get naked for me," I told him. As I tossed my bra aside, my brain went click-click-click, and then I imagined the noise again as he unzipped his fly to reveal a proud cock, gorgeous and veiny and already weeping with need.

The rest of the night, that sound was never far from my mind. Click-click-click as I took him deep. Click-click-click as I gripped his shoulders for balance and sweated. Click-click-click as we changed positions and I settled onto my hands and knees. Click-click-click as I suckled his softened cock through a moment of peace.

As it got later, I convinced Jonas to admit to more of his secret desires. Click-click-click as I showed him how I touch myself. Click-click-click as I probed his ass with one gentle finger. Click-click-click as he licked the webbing between my toes.

When morning came, it was as if we'd spent a lifetime together. I tugged him to his feet and slung my arm over his back as we watched the sun spread delicate dawn bruises over the sky. I pressed a kiss to Jonas's cheek and promised that I would text him if I ever came to Burlington again, and I hoped he understood that I meant it.

He embraced me, his fingers gripping my ass hard enough to hurt, but then he did as I'd asked and let me go. He remained silent as I drove him back to his car, but as he stepped out, he nodded and gave me a soft smile. I watched him until he drove away, and I thought there was something different about his gait. I wondered if mine had changed as well.

Then, I headed back for the cabin. I was tired from everything I'd done with Jonas, but for me the morning held more than falling action. My cell phone waited on the kitchen table where I'd left it. My thighs clenched as I anticipated finally finding out what Ron thought of all this.

I prevented myself from running into the house. There was no cool to my walk, though, and I fumbled the keys twice trying to get in the front door. The phone seemed to take forever to start up, and I tapped my foot impatiently as it played music and displayed graphics and searched for a network.

Ron's first set of texts appeared. *Hello, baby. You look smoking in that leather jacket. And you know just where to stand. Either that, or there's no such thing as bad lighting as far as you're concerned.* I bit my lip. Normally, I would have answered that, flirting back. I didn't want to have hurt him with my silence.

Scrolling through, my evening replayed in phases. *So you're not answering me this time? But I see that wicked look in your eyes. This is how you want to play it?*

Later: *That boy has no idea what he's getting into.* He really had been with me all night. It warmed my heart to know I hadn't invented my sense of our connection.

And after that, no texts at all for hours. Hopefully because Ron's fingers had been too busy with his camera. At the very bottom of my phone's log was Ron's final text, sent only a few minutes before. *Fuck. I just about lost my mind last night.*

There was nothing else. Ron had to know I fucked other people. I'd never pretended to be celibate or exclusive. This was, however, the first time I'd fucked someone during one of "our" weekends, and my heart pounded as I hoped I hadn't miscalculated. I'd wanted to take things further with Ron, not drive him away.

I was barely able to look at my phone's screen as I texted my reply. *You okay?*

Ron must have been waiting. He answered in seconds. *I need to see you.*

I still didn't know if that was good or bad, but I couldn't take time to think. I stepped outside.

The trees rustled. A man's shape appeared. After everything we'd been through, I expected him to seem familiar, but he didn't. For a moment, we just stared at each other, eye to eye for the first time, no camera lens between us.

He was younger than I'd thought, and darker and slimmer. If he'd been at the bar the night before, I would have chosen him. I supposed that his taste for old-school camera gear had made me imagine an older man, gone to seed. The man before me was in his prime, however, vitality radiating from his eyes, so full of artistry that it seemed to have burst out of his body and manifested on his skin in the form of vibrant tattoos.

"Show me your pussy," he commanded.

My cunt thrummed as I stripped for him. His gaze hit my skin with more intensity than a slap. I trembled. Gripping my labia, I spread myself for him. Ron stepped closer.

I didn't know if he was going to touch me, or if he wanted to fuck me now. I wasn't sure if I wanted that to happen. I liked him as a voyeur, and what we had was working. I didn't want it to change; I just wanted more of it.

It was hard to breathe as he approached, closer and closer, so much silence between us that I imagined I could hear grass stalks bending under his black boots.

"Open it wider," Ron whispered. "I want to see what you look like freshly fucked."

I did as he ordered and couldn't resist brushing a finger over my clit, making myself shudder. There was a click-click-click. I glanced up in surprise, and there was the camera I'd been thinking of all night, as if straight out of my imagination, and the noise of it was real, not just in my head.

"Keep it up, baby," Ron said. "Make that pussy quiver for me."

I gave a big exhale and leaned back against the cabin's outer wall. I put two hands on my cunt, one pressing fingers inside and the other teasing my clit. Click-click-click. Click-click-click. Ron and I stared each other down, and I felt full of him, connected to him, understood by him. There was no need to speak. He could see everything I needed him to see.

Orgasm took me, and Ron was right there with me, his focus close on my pussy, his camera saying click-click-click.

STAR FUCKER

Malin James

"Star fucker."

I barely look up. "Star fucker" is one of Jane's favorite insults. It's gotten a lot of play recently—almost as much as "useless douche." But "star fucker" is special. If "useless douche" were a pair of granny heels, "star fucker" would be stilettos. Jane's virtuosic scorn twists and hardens the *r*'s so that it sounds more like "st*rrrr* fuck*rrrr*" by the time it leaves her mouth.

"St*rrrrr* fuck*rrrr*."

She says it again. For emphasis. Jane is good at scorn. She always has been. I think she'd shrivel up without it. She's an agent, after all—balls and scorn have fueled her career. But then, of course, you know that. Jane is your agent. And the girl, the st*rrrrr* fuck*rrrr*, who has been judged not once, but twice with enough scorn to kill a Borgia, is hanging off your arm.

"Jesus fucking Christ," she says, shoving her drink at me. "Viv, I'll be right back."

I nod, and take a sip. I'm not really paying attention. This party isn't how I'd have chosen to spend my last evening in town, but unless you're into celebrities, Hollywood isn't paradise to begin with. I'm mostly immune to celebrities. Mostly. There is one exception. But then, you know that too.

I scan the busy bar, looking for Jane. She might be five foot one, but her presence is huge. It's only a second before I see her, bearing down on a man whose back is to the room. Her shoulders are set like a boxer's. Our grandma would be proud. Meanwhile, her target is disentangling himself from a slinky little blonde. The s*trrr* fuck*rrrr*, I presume.

The blonde pouts in the parody of a come-on—hips cocked, breasts pert, no underwire needed. The man regretfully shakes his head just as Jane the Mighty arrives. Apparently delighted, the man swings her up like a rag doll until she whacks him on the arm. The blonde slinks away as he laughs and puts her down. And that's when I see his face—*your* face—clearly for the first time.

Michael Spencer.

Jesus fucking Christ.

I nearly drop Jane's drink. You are the exception to my celebrity thing. I am not immune to you.

My belly contracts as I look at your face. It's not perfect or even handsome, but it is charismatic—so goddamn charismatic that I want to fuck you right now, and I'm not usually a fuck-you-right-now kind of girl, but it's a full-court press. My brain and my body are fully on board.

I swallow the rest of Jane's drink. My tongue feels lush and nimble and my lady-bits are slick. You're still across the room and I am one hot mess.

You bend and say something to Jane. Then, nodding, she hauls you across the room. It takes me a second to realize that she's hauling you to me. I panic. I want to bolt, but I can't work out an escape. My brain has checked out. Lust has made me dumb.... I feel like a useless douche.

"Viv. There you are."

Wishing I'd had more booze, I plaster on a smile and turn around. And there you are, standing with Jane, looking tall and lean and so damn easy in your suit. My mouth opens and closes. Then it opens again, and I know I look like a fish.

"Viv," Jane says, waiting a beat. "Hello? You okay?"

"Yeah," I say, brightly. "Yeah. I'm great."

I'm just deeply, deeply in lust with the man standing next to you.

"Good. Then I can introduce you. Michael Spencer, this is my sister, Vivian Martel. Viv, this is Spence."

Jane looks at me expectantly, like I'm supposed to shake your hand, which is an act of science fiction in the genre of my life. I do, however, manage an eloquent nod. Then, like a normal, functioning person, you smile and extend your hand. My heart thumps. I feel besieged.

"Nice to meet you, Viv. Can I call you Viv? It's how Jane refers to you, so that's what I call you in my head."

You call me in your head....

I start to say, "of course," but it turns into "uh." I try something simpler instead.

"Yes."

I nod to drive my point home.

"Then you can call me Spence."

You're smiling. It's my turn to talk now, but your hand is still on mine. I want to bring it to my lips. I want to taste and suck and lick, and I'm frozen because I know this would be in extremely poor taste. I feel Jane shift, impatiently. My weirdness is weirding her out. Pull it together, Viv....

"You're, uh...much taller than I thought."

Jane gives me a what-the-fuck look. You respond with an easy grin.

"Yeah, I get that a lot."

Slight pressure on my hand. I am utterly charmed. Jane snorts.

"Spence, let go of her hand."

Sheepishly, you do. My fingers are warm and tingly and I feel, quite literally, weak in the knees. This is getting out of hand. Tired of being ridiculous, I look straight into your eyes, which, I can tell you, is not easy to do. They are dark blue and lovely, and they crinkle at the edges, as if you smile with them a lot. You're smiling with them now.

To my relief, I don't point this out.

"So," Jane says, dousing the situation with a bucket of common sense. "Do you remember how I mentioned that one of my clients loved your book? Well, that was Spence. He wants to talk to you about optioning it. He's been hounding me for months."

To my shock, you blush bright red. My brain comes back from vacation and I kick it into gear.

"Thanks, Jane. You couldn't have told me before?"

Jane looks at me, unimpressed. "I'm telling you now, Viv." Then she takes the empty glass from my hand and rattles the lonely cubes. "Lush." She shakes her head. "Now, if you'll excuse me, I need to get a drink. You two have fun."

"But..."

Jane cuts me off with a fantastically obvious wink.

"Chat. I'll be back in a bit."

Then she barrels away like a juggernaut aimed at the bar. The crowd parts as if God had decreed it.

"So," you say, watching her go. "Has she always been like that?"

"You mean bossy, pushy and blunt? Yeah, pretty much."

I smile. My hand is still warm from your touch.

That wink was Jane's blessing. I can go after you if I want to. Unquestionably, I do. But now that we're alone I don't know where to start. Do you even want to be pursued? I look up at your face, which is, adorably, still a bit red. Possibly you do.... You scan my face as your hips turn, very slightly, toward mine. Then your eyes drop to my lips. My breath catches. Yes. I think you do...

You're perfect, I want to tell you. You can take the rights. I based the lead on you. On you, on you, on you...

"I'm so glad we—"

"It's so good to—"

We stop, laughing predictably. We're a cliché, and I don't even mind.

"Sorry," you say. "After you."

Your voice is rich, with a soft, rounded clip. I want to strip off my clothes and feel that richness drifting over my skin. Of course, I don't tell you this.

"It's lovely to meet you," I murmur instead. Now, it's my turn to blush. "I'm... I'm a great fan of your work."

My blush gets worse because it's true. If it weren't, I wouldn't be panting like a fangirl. I'd have thought that this would be safe to assume, but you honestly look a bit thrown.

"I could say the same of you."

You reach out and brush my arm. The contact is strictly platonic, but I have never, ever, in my entire life been so pain-fully turned on.

"The thing is that I—"

"Hi again, Spence!"

It's the slinky, star-fucker blonde. Your mouth hardens—a subtle change but it speaks volumes. Suddenly, I feel like Jane.

"Hello..." you say, trailing off. You're polite, but you make it clear that you don't remember her name.

"Geneva," she supplies, smiling, as her hand flutters to her chest. "You know, like the country—remember?"

"Actually," I say, aiming for conversational and coming up short. "I think Geneva might be a city. They had a convention there once."

You look at me, eyes crinkling. Geneva is not impressed.

"Oh?" she says, cocking a hip. "How interesting. And who are you?"

"This is Vivian Martel," you say, smoothly cutting in.

Geneva inspects me, visibly noting the way your hand is hovering over my hip. She pastes on a sticky smile, in deference, I'm sure, to you.

"So, what do you do?"

"I'm a writer," I say, suppressing a grin. I love answering that question in L.A. Geneva perks right up.

"Really? Film or TV?"

"Books," I reply.

"Books?"

"Books."

"Oh. Well. I guess that's cool."

Skeptically, she turns back to you. "So, my friend and I are leaving, and we were wondering..."

She leans forward, dishing out the goods.

St*rrrr* fuck*rrrr*.

"If you might want to come with us."

You smile, looking almost regretful, as you skillfully dodge her breasts. "Thanks so much but no."

"Oh..." Geneva pouts. "Well, maybe some other time."

Biting her lip like a tart, she snags a napkin from a waiter and, using your chest as a writing surface, jots down her number before tucking it into the breast pocket of your shirt. Then she winks and walks away.

Awkwardly, we watch her go. I'm amused, but your absolute lack of expression drains the smile from my face. Suddenly, almost violently, my attraction to you shifts, and I no longer want a film star. Suddenly, I just want you.

"Listen," you say, turning to me. "That isn't... Look, do you want to leave?"

You're blushing a little again.

"Yes. I really do."

We sneak out of the party like a couple of kids cutting class. Then we head down the hall to the elevators. We still haven't kissed, but we're going to. That much is pretty clear.

You hit the DOWN button, and stand close as we wait, so close that your knuckles brush the back of my hand. Our fingers lace lightly, back to back, as we stare straight ahead, right into our reflection in the soft, polished brass. We look old-fashioned and lovely. You're lovely, I think. By the time the doors open, my thighs are slick and I can barely breathe.

"After you."

Your voice is husky as our fingers drift apart. I step into the little brass box, unable to respond.

25...24...23...

The floors tick by as our bodies angle and sway, silently negotiating the terms of our attraction. We're playing with the tension, pulling it, teasing, seeing how thin it will go.

22...21...

Your hand drifts down to the base of my spine before cupping the small of my back. Desire seeps through me, coating my skin, as I arch into the flat of your hand.

20...19...18...

Your mouth is close. We are so close. My bones go soft as your fingers drift lower and stop just short of my rump.

17…16…

Our hips meet and the bulge of your erection brushes up against my mound. And that's it. I'm done. I'm not going to wait. I smack the emergency button and find your hungry mouth.

The elevator jolts to a stop as I breathe you in. You taste as good as you smell—clean and crisp, like expensive champagne. It's the last thing I think before I start to undo your belt.

You groan, kissing me back with your famous mouth as you press me hard against the wall. Then you shrug off your jacket and slip your hand up my skirt before pulling my panties down. I gasp, as my belly contracts. I'm already soaking wet. You make a noise deep in your chest. Then your fingers find my pussy and begin to stroke. My breasts ache, everything aches. I'm starving for your cock. Desperate and shaky, I quickly unzip your pants.

"Jesus," I breathe, as I draw down your briefs. Your cock is gorgeous—full and thick and impossibly hard, with a glistening, swollen head. I stroke it—I can't help it—and you wince as your hips thrust into my hand. I am full of the impulse to suck. You must read it in me because you quickly bear my weight.

"Later," you whisper. Your voice is raw. "We have to hurry, Viv."

I know, I know, I know.

Every inch of me wants you—breasts, pussy, skin, lungs. Still standing, I spread my legs for you as you slide your cock between my thighs and rub your shaft against my cunt.

"Hurry, Spence. Please."

I can barely see straight. I can barely breathe. You get a condom out from I don't-know-where and then you take your cock, still slick with my juice, and slide the condom on. I'm swollen and gaping as you pick me up and grip my ass with your hands. You're shaking. I'm shaking. My legs wrap around your waist. Then you kiss me as you thrust.

We're mad. We fuck madly. I have never felt so greedy. You batter me, devoid of your famous finesse as I arch and writhe and claw torturously toward my peak.

Then the elevator shudders. With a jerk, we start to move.

15...14...

"Spence," I cry. My voice breaks and you grunt. You know, but we're not going to stop.

13...12...11...

The elevator slows and drifts to a natural halt.

"Son of a bitch," you breathe. Then you bury yourself in me, right to the hilt and slam the button that keeps the doors closed. They struggle, attempting to open, but you jam the button hard, while my pussy flutters and pulses around your static cock.

I'll admit that I'm impressed by your presence of mind, but most of me just wants to come, so I take up the rhythm and circle my hips as the elevator stops struggling and finally moves on.

10...9...

The orgasm starts to skitter along the edge of my nerves, firing through my limbs.

8...7...6...

I'm grinding against you, and I'm painfully close. You instinctively change the angle of your thrust, grazing my G-spot with your head as you circle my clit with your thumb. I shriek, and the orgasm that was just a shimmer before explodes through me like a bomb.

5...

I arch against you, gripping, clutching, mewling like a cat. It would be humiliating and unthinkable if you weren't moaning and panting too. But, oh my god, you are. So the orgasm washes over me in wave after wave, as your thrusts come fast and desperate. Your breath catches and your eyes glaze over. Loose-hipped and receptive, my legs tighten around your waist. Then you come, groaning as you kiss me hard enough to bruise.

4...

Gently, you lower me down to my feet, as my orgasm pulses and ebbs. My body craves more. It's desperate for more.

3...

But we are officially out of time. I straighten my dress and snatch up your jacket as you buckle up your belt.

2...1...

The doors begin to open. On cue, my panties fall out from a fold in your jacket. You catch them midair and grin.

Two women are waiting to get on. It's Geneva and her friend. We smile as they take us both in. My lipstick is all over your mouth. You look adorable. We're rumpled and flushed and the elevator smells, undeniably, of sex.

They ignore you and look at me.

"Star fucker," they murmur, scornfully.

I smile.

Oh, yes, my girl. I am.

THE ART TEACHER

Rachel Woe

Every art classroom I've ever been in smells the same: the pungent, intoxicating aroma of tempera and acrylic paints; the dry, woody perfume of construction paper; the acrid bite of paint thinner combined with old-building staples like dust and black mold. Mr. Thompson's room is no different, though I can just barely detect the lingering scent of coffee wafting out from his cluttered office where he sits, reclining in a creaky, ragged desk chair, scribbling grades into a tattered binder. I long to be back there with him. I can imagine myself sauntering in, closing the door behind me, peeling off my clothes and begging him to do whatever he wants with me.

I want him to be my first. Yes, he's fourteen years my senior and if anyone found out he'd most certainly be fired and maybe even serve prison time, but my adolescent heart wants what it wants. It wants him. It wants his wide palms and long fingers moving over my skin, his mouth upon mine, his groin pressed against my backside, his cock—well, this is where it gets a bit hazy. I've seen porn and R-rated movies and I know what happens when people have sex, but since I've only ever gone as far as French kissing, I have nothing tangible to relate to, nothing to flesh out that void in my fantasies.

Today I have chosen to remain after school to work on my final project for the big senior art show next Friday that the department puts on every year. I'm in the process of painting a life-sized portrait of a woman, naked against a stark, black background. She is beautiful and imperfect and stylized to the point of surreality, but still identifiable as a woman.

Mr. Thompson says I am very talented and that he would be happy to write a recommendation for me to any art school of my choosing, should I wish to pursue this work professionally. I told him I would think about it. As far as I'm concerned, anything that allows me more time alone with him is worth pursuing.

I hear papers shuffling and the creak of his office chair, followed by footsteps and the uneven spray of water sputtering out of the old faucet where we cleanse our brushes and palettes. He is in the classroom now, maybe twenty feet behind me.

I am standing at a long table where I have laid out an assortment of paints and other tools, as well as my work-in-progress. I bend over the metal slab and roll onto the balls of my feet so that my ass is slightly raised and my back arched. I hope I'm not being too obvious in my short skirt, gray stockings with rose detailing and black tank top. Technically, we aren't supposed to wear tank tops to school, but since it's after hours and I'm growing bored with subtlety, I've removed my sweatshirt so that Mr. Thompson can get a better look at my sizable chest and petite figure. I'm no model by any stretch of the imagination, but puberty has been surprisingly kind to me, so although I may stand almost a foot shorter than him, I am well proportioned. More than anything, I hope he notices this, too.

I've hiked the skirt up a bit so that when I bend over, one can just barely see a hint of my purple knickers. I've always loved that word; it's naughtier than underwear and less trite than panties. The fact that I'm not British is of little concern to me.

The faucet squeaks and then there is silence. I assume he's still at the counter but don't dare turn to look. I pray to every god and goddess that has ever existed that he is noticing me: the hint of purple fabric, how the lace trim on my stockings clings to the flesh of my upper thighs. Of course, there's always the possibility that he's eyeing me with disdain, thinking my efforts silly or too transparent. I would die if he asked me to cover up. Then again, I would die if he asked me to take it off. Please, just fucking kill me already.

Mr. Thompson's footsteps break the silence, growing louder as he meanders over to the table. My heart threatens to choke me, but I remain composed. He is standing beside me, surveying my work. I happen to be shading the woman's left breast, relying on neon yellows and navy blues to give it a more three-dimensional appearance.

"This is coming along beautifully, Mireille. I really like how you've decided to go with unconventional colors. They stand out nicely against the black background." He gestures to the work I've already completed around her face, those lean, beautiful hands moving in ways that both thrill and transfix. I can't help but relish the way my name expertly rolls off of his tongue; he obviously speaks French.

"Thanks." I am nervous and can't seem to raise my voice above a loud whisper but the emptiness of the room negates the need to project myself.

"Do you think you'll have it ready by next Friday?" His gray-blue eyes follow the brush as it strokes the underside of the painted woman's breast.

Mr. Thompson does not look at me, which I find to be both a blessing and a tragedy. I watch him longer than I should, marveling at the sharpness of his cheekbones and the angle of his jaw, all painfully untouchable.

"I think so. The outline is finished. All I have left to do is the shading."

He glances at me and my groin tightens. I bite the interior of my cheek to distract myself and avert my eyes back down toward the painting; the woman's stare mocks me.

"Well, let me know if I can help in any way." Mr. Thompson turns and retraces his steps to the office.

My thoughts race as I think of all the things I'd like him to help me with. For starters, he might help me out of my skirt and stockings. After which he could help himself to my virgin cunt—damn, I love that word. My mother absolutely cannot abide hearing it but I use it every chance I get.

Cunt. My tight, virgin cunt. My hungry cunt.

I really must stop before I lose my composure, as I've already begun squeezing my thighs together and rocking back and forth reflexively. The fact that I have to urinate only draws more attention to that sadly neglected area. It's not that I do not masturbate, because I do—often—but I've never had another person besides my family doctor touch me there. It's one thing to do it yourself, to have complete control over which areas get stimulated and in what way, but I can only imagine how exciting and scary it would be to have someone else's hands, fingers, and—oh fuck—mouth down there, manipulating me in ways I can't even conceptualize.

The shriek of a telephone in Mr. Thompson's office jolts me out of my reverie and I realize that I've just accidentally over-shaded the painted woman's right breast.

"Shit," I hiss, dipping my brush into a bit of yellow in the hopes of compensating for the damage.

Mr. Thompson answers the phone at a normal volume but then begins to speak in hushed whispers. I hear footsteps and then the sound of a heavy door creaking and latching. I turn and see that he has closed the door to his office. At the same time, I notice a quarter-sized hole beneath the knob. The door must have featured a lock at one point but, for whatever reason, it was removed. I debate the ethics of grasping this opportunity to spy on him and my curiosity is far more powerful than any sense of morality. Before long, I'm removing my gray flats and slinking toward the door.

I crouch, hovering just above the floor with my eye to the peephole. I can barely make out his side of the conversation and am both affronted and intrigued by what I hear.

"Of course I've thought about you since August. How could I not? That was some of the best damn head I've ever gotten."

He is talking to a woman. I know this because the tinny, unintelligible voice coming out the other end of the phone sounds high pitched, feminine. His own voice is low and guttural, deeper than I'm used to hearing in class. I'm both insanely jealous and eager to hear more.

Mr. Thompson is reclining in his desk chair with his legs spread wide and his other hand stuffed inside the pocket of his paint-stained jeans. There is some squeaky dialogue from the other end of the line. I wish I could hear what she's saying, as he's obviously enjoying the conversation. The thought of myself ever being the catalyst for that broad, lascivious smile on his face makes my cunt throb.

"I'm glad I was able to do that for you."

He pauses, listening, then continues, "If I could, I'd drive up there this weekend and finish you off properly."

More muffled dialogue, then, "Nah, I have this art show thing to get ready for so I'll be pretty busy till next weekend.

Believe me, I'd much rather spend the next three days with my head between your legs."

A sly smile spreads across his face. "Oh, really? Well, you're welcome to try. Hold on a sec."

Mr. Thompson rises up and begins to walk toward the door. I scramble to the opposite side of the heavy demonstration table by the sinks, my stocking-clad feet aiding in my haste. He opens the door and peers out into the classroom. My things are still scattered across the long table but I am sufficiently hidden from sight. He closes the door and retreats back into his office, most likely assuming that I've stepped out to use the bathroom or acquire food. I quietly make my way back to the door and its glorious peephole.

I hear the clinking of his belt being unfastened before my eye can focus. With one hand, he unbuttons his jeans and draws the zipper down over an enormous bulge in the front of his pants. I am mesmerized, having never seen a man's penis in person before besides my father's, which glimpses only occurred on a handful of occasions and were always accidental—and it was never erect.

Mr. Thompson reaches into the front of his pants and pulls it out. I gasp and then chide myself, afraid he might have heard me, but he is preoccupied, making encouraging, breathy noises into the phone's receiver. He strokes his cock, which is long, thick and smooth, almost picture perfect. No stranger to the Internet, I have a general idea of what an ideal erection is supposed to look like: tan at the base, thick, and growing pinker toward the head. The head itself is bulbous but not overly so; big enough to intimidate a novice like me, yet, my eyes are glued to it. From what I've read and from what my friends have told me, I can deduce that he's uncircumcised, but that the foreskin is wrapped quite tightly around his shaft, peeling back behind the rose-colored head with ease.

I want to wrap my fingers around it. I want to feel it inside me.

Mr. Thompson continues to run his hand up and down, gently stretching the foreskin, whispering, "Mmm," and "Go on," as he squeezes and milks his formidable cock. I wonder if it's warm and what it tastes like and, before long, I find my hand cupping my cunt through my skirt, clutching and massaging in rhythm with his slow, deliberate strokes.

"I'd like that." He growls, breathing heavily. "I want to taste your pussy. I want to shove my tongue in slow and deep, right as you're about to come."

I can barely contain my own rapid breathing as I slide my hand under my skirt, finding my knickers damp and my clit so hard that I can feel it through the thin fabric. My god, this man is so beautiful and obviously an attentive lover, the way he talks about going down on this woman. I want him to go down on me. I want him to plant his mouth on my cunt and let his tongue roam over my most sensitive bits.

Mr. Thompson proceeds to pump his cock, lingering on the now glistening, pink head every few strokes, his pelvis thrusting upward into his palm. His eyes are closed and his mouth slightly open, as he pants and moans for the woman on the other end of the line. For a brief moment, I hate her, whoever she is. Then, in a split second, I am so overwhelmingly grateful to her and whatever she's saying to make him put on such a gorgeous, inadvertent display.

"Yeah, I know how you like it," he says. "You want me to bend you over and fuck you from behind and that's exactly what I'm going to do. Right in your tight, wet pussy."

The mental imagery of him doing the same to me is so delicious that I have to consciously restrain myself from barging in, grabbing his cock and begging him to fuck my poor, deprived cunt. I can't take the indirect pressure any longer, so I slip my fingers beneath the elastic of my knickers and caress my clit, which is moist and beyond sensitive. Even now, I am close to coming, so I take precautions and cover my mouth with my other hand. I watch his strokes become faster, tighter, less controlled, up and down over that gorgeous monstrosity that I would give anything to have fill me up and split me in two.

"Come for me," he whispers.

I can just make out the sound of the woman's shrill cries as she is undoubtedly overtaken by thoughts of Mr. Thompson and his perfect cock. My arm begins to grow tired and my legs ache from crouching but I do not cease fingering myself. Each stroke of his hand whets my appetite further. I slip a finger into my dripping cunt, imagining that it's him, and proceed to fuck myself. True, my finger barely matches his girth but it is all I have. I attempt two fingers now, which would normally be too much for my virgin pussy to take, but I am so unbelievably wet that they slip inside with ease.

My eye darts from his now magenta-tinted cock to his beautiful face, open mouthed and just as flushed. I imagine myself perched on his lap, my warmth enveloping him, impaled and enflamed, as I thrust two fingers in and out of my sopping twat.

Mr. Thompson pauses for a second to lick his palm and I see that the skin on his cock is taut and bulging with purple veins. It is bigger and harder than it was even a moment ago, and I can't help but whimper at the sight of it. I don't care how much it might hurt, I want it inside me, stretching me, tearing my hymen and transforming me into a woman—the kind who can make a man come with just her words and imagination. He resumes his pumping and I return my fingers to my aching clit, which is almost too sensitive at this point. I press on, so close to an orgasm that I can already feel it building inside, threatening to topple me from my low perch.

"Oh god, I'm coming. I'm coming!" he moans, probably a little louder than he should.

His hand motions slow as he makes one final pelvic thrust and I witness spurt after spurt of thick, white semen shoot out of him and onto his hand and T-shirt. He rubs himself slower and slower, until finally, breathless and spent, he lets his cock fall limp onto his semen-stained shirt, his hand hanging limp in his lap.

I'm quickly overtaken by my own orgasm, pulsating and spreading out from my cunt all the way up my spine and into the base of my brain via delightful vibrations that echo out into my fingers and toes. I clumsily fall back onto the linoleum, staring at the tiled ceiling until I hear the creak of his desk chair.

Shit.

I clamber up off the floor and glide back over to the table where the painted woman eyes me knowingly.

"Don't judge me," I whisper.

Thinking that it will look strange that I haven't made any progress since we last spoke, I quickly snatch the painting and carry it over to the drying rack, placing it toward the bottom where it won't be easily noticed. I grab my palate and brushes and carry them over to the sink and begin rinsing the paint out of the bristles while, at the same time, washing the juices from my fingers.

After a few minutes, Mr. Thompson opens the door and emerges wearing a different T-shirt. He is startled to see me but stifles his reaction, no doubt in an effort to appear nonchalant.

"Oh, Mireille, you're still here." He glances in my direction but avoids making eye contact, running his now clean fingers through his hair: a nervous habit.

"I went to grab a drink and then came back to finish up the torso. I should really get going, though. I'm sure the extracurricular bus will be leaving soon." I wash the last of the paint off my palette and then set it onto the counter to dry.

"Well, if you miss it, I can give you a ride home." He smiles warily at my feet, raising his eyes to mine for only a brief second before darting them away.

"That would be great."

I walk back over to my station to collect the paints I'd been using, depositing them into their appropriate receptacles in the "Acrylic" closet. Mr. Thompson disappears into his office and I begin to gather my things. As cold as it will be outside, I refrain from wearing my sweatshirt, thinking that perhaps he will notice that I'd been sweating and put two and two together.

Then again, do I want him to know that I was watching him or that I heard his conversation?

As awkward as I feel about violating his privacy, I still can't help myself. I love him. I don't really know what any of that means at eighteen, but it feels right to think it. When he laughs, my pulse dances; when he smiles, my whole body melts; when he touches himself, I wish our palms could trade places. He is the most beautiful thing I have ever seen and if all I ever get from him is the stolen recollection of his enraptured face as he masturbates himself to completion, then I will take it.

Mr. Thompson emerges from his office wearing a light jacket and a brown messenger bag slung across his chest. "It's almost five. I might as well just drive you," he says.

I nod, heading toward the door of the classroom as he turns off the fluorescent lights.

"You'll probably want your shoes."

I raise my eyebrow, confused.

He points. "By your workstation."

Glancing back at the table, I see my flats lying by the stool where I'd tossed them just before creeping over to spy on him. "Oh, right. Thanks." I slip them on.

"Shall we?" He gestures for me to lead the way down the side stairwell and out into the teacher's parking lot.

I've seen Mr. Thompson's car from a distance but never before had the privilege of riding in it. He unlocks my side first and holds the door open for me. I smile shyly and duck inside as he closes the door behind me. I can't quite put my finger on exactly what the interior of his car smells like, but it's not unpleasant. Something like pine with a hint of stale coffee; he loves his coffee.

He opens the driver's side door and plants himself in the front seat, a mere ten inches from me. I am paralyzed. If I wanted to, I could reach out and touch him. I notice that my panties are still wet with my juices and worry about leaving a damp spot on his seat cushion.

Mr. Thompson tosses his bag into the backseat, revs the engine and turns on the heat. "It'll be warmer soon. This car has a decent heating system, unlike my last one."

I nod.

"So, where do you live?" he asks.

I clear my throat. "Fifty-six Butler Terrace. About ten minutes from here. Just take a right onto Fergus and then keep going till you hit Roosevelt Ave., on the left. Then take a right at the stop sign."

"Ah, I know where that is. My brother used to live off of Roosevelt. Buckle up, please."

I reach for the seat belt, my shaky hands making it difficult to achieve a decent grip. He smiles affectionately and reaches across my seat, deftly yanking the belt over my chest and snapping it into place. My cheeks betray me.

"Thanks," I mumble.

"Not a problem." Glancing over his shoulder, he backs out of the parking space and commences the short ride to my house. We sit in silence for a few moments until he decides to switch on the radio. The car fills with the intellectual babble of NPR as I keep my eyes firmly fixed on the road ahead.

"Sorry I, uh, disappeared for a bit. I had to take a phone call." His voice is even but I recognize the slight change in pitch on the last two words: phone call.

"That's okay," I say, stealing a quick glance in his direction.

"I just feel—since I offered to help you earlier—it may have been rude of me to then make myself unavailable."

Our eyes meet for a brief second and I immediately realize what his game is. He is trying to determine whether or not I heard anything while he was pleasuring himself in the back room.

In that moment, it occurs to me that our dynamic has changed. Right now, in this vehicle, I am the one with the power. If I say nothing, he will either assume that I didn't hear anything or that I am ignorant. If I confront him, then he'll be burdened with the task of convincing me that it was something else or be forced to come clean and beg for my discretion.

If today were any other day, I might have opted to keep my mouth shut, to deny any knowledge of what happened behind that office door. But something transpired between us and that heavy slab of wood. Watching this man overcome with desire—losing himself in the sensuality of that mystery woman's voice and the imagery she fed him—awoke something inside me. Contained within her voice was an awe-inspiring amount of feminine sexual power, so much so that he was positively enslaved to it.

Why couldn't I wield such power?

Halted beneath the glow of a red light against the impending dusk, I can feel him studying me. I turn to look at him, forcing myself to maintain eye contact. We stare at each other: him, growing increasingly unsettled and me, slowly becoming aware of my own authority.

A loud honk from the car behind us forces Mr. Thompson to turn his attention to the fresh green light. I take a deep breath before responding, just as we are about to turn onto my street.

"I notice you changed your shirt after taking that phone call." I watch him bristle at this observation. "Tell me, do come stains wash out easily or will you have to toss the shirt?"

His eyes open wider than I've ever seen them as his lips purse into a thin line. He is speechless.

"Oh, this one is me," I gesture to the house we just passed.

Mr. Thompson brakes and we lurch forward. Still dumbstruck, he turns toward me, a look of mortification coloring his gorgeous features.

"Don't worry, I won't tell anyone," I say, unbuckling my seat belt.

With my eyes firmly fixed on his and my legs slightly spread, I slowly raise the hem of my skirt above my cunt. His gaze lowers and he watches me, unmoving, swallowing hard. I take hold of the waistband of my knickers and, raising my ass off the seat a bit, slide them down my thighs, over my stockings, and off my feet.

Mr. Thompson's eyes are trained on my cunt, still moist and glistening. I lift my underwear up off the floor with one finger, dangling them at eye-level for a few seconds before dropping them into his lap, which, if I'm not mistaken, is now sporting a hint of that familiar bulge. He glances down at the bundle of cloth, drenched in all the right places, and then back at me, conflicted.

"See you in class, Mr. Thompson."

His mouth parts as if he is about to respond but emits no

sound. I drape my skirt back over my thighs and exit the vehicle, leaving him stupefied and visibly aroused.

As I round the car and begin backtracking down the street toward my house, the light wind lifting my skirt to kiss my exposed cunt, I can't help but notice small, subtle hints of newfound confidence. My stride is longer, my hips more prone to swaying, my shoulders naturally held back and my posture straight and extended. Is this a taste of what it feels like to be a full-fledged, sexually assertive woman? If so, I can only imagine the transformation that awaits once I actually have sex.

Perhaps I can ask Mr. Thompson for a private tutoring session.

GWENDOLYN AND MARIO
GO TO PHILADELPHIA

Gwendolyn Kansen

We congregated in Peter Salisbury's room one Friday night in early October, right before it got cold. Teresa was pressed up next to him as usual, telling us about the newest slash she was writing.

"Okay, so Brock is second in line for the state wrestling championships, and Steven tells him that there's only one way he can beat the contender." As always, Peter was tremendously patient with her so he could go on being adored. She was what he needed. I was sitting on the floor pressing a cheese-flavored Bugle onto each of my fingers wondering who had worse Asperger's, me or him.

I went out to the bathrooms and heard clambering up the stairs in the hall. A drunk, grinning Mario Vincento skipped up to me and grabbed my shoulders.

"How's Cody?" I said dryly.

"He's great! He gave me some Goldschläger."

"Nice."

One of the basketball players walked by in his towel and winked at me. A door slammed down the hall. I could hear Peter in his room. He was now continuing his anti–Hillary Clinton vendetta. This time he was ranting about how Bill Clinton had voted to take money away from the Navy.

"I'm so happy to see you, Gwendolyn!" drunk Mario continued. "I want to go somewhere with you. Just you and me."

Peter's voice bounced from down the hall: "He must have been too busy having sexual relations with that woman to think about how the average sergeant makes less than most strippers!"

"It has to be somewhere neither of us has ever been to before," I said, thinking that if I christened a new city with Mario he'd see how captivating I was. "Pittsburgh and Philadelphia are pretty close."

"I've always wanted to see Philadelphia!" Mario exclaimed. He jumped up and ran into Peter's room and yelled "Who wants to come with us to Philadelphia?"

"What? You're not going anywhere! You're too drunk!" Peter boomed.

"Maybe you could come with us and drive," I offered, hoping he'd say no.

"I'm not going to Philadelphia! And you're going to bed!"

"How about we go in the morning?" I suggested.

"You suck, Peter," Mario whined as he poured himself another cup of Goldschläger.

He staggered back into his room, and I went back to Potter Hall. I crawled under my comforter and fell asleep with what must have been a totem pole–sized grin, thinking about how many cool points I had now that I was doing something completely spontaneous and 100 percent orchestrated by me.

* * *

The next morning at nine, I put on my red leather skirt and red sandals, and my red, white and blue rugby-style shirt from H&M. For the club I brought my pink-and-green silk chiffon dress from Chaiken that I'd found for six dollars in the sale bin at Annie Creamcheese in Georgetown. Mario was wearing sunglasses, his trademark Aeropostale polo shirt and his favorite black jeans when he picked me up. I marched into the dining hall and stuffed some fruit into the Styrofoam container. Then we were on our way.

All of Mecklenville looked better that morning as we left it. I watched happy people walking in and out of the shops buying five-toed shoes and beads and essential oils. The snapped wooden rafters on the abandoned farmhouse right outside town looked like they were glistening, and I smiled out the window at the crows poking around looking for corn. As we hit the highway, Mario turned on the radio and we danced in our seats to the music. "You're so funny I love you!" he yelled over Timbaland's "The Way I Are." Two hours went by and we stopped at Havre de Grace's Maryland House, where I bought each of us a flashing key chain.

The first thing I noticed about Philadelphia is that it's just the right size. It isn't oppressively huge and there weren't an unmanageable number of people on the sidewalks. The architecture is beautiful and there are a lot of parks. Each neighborhood is separate and distinct.

There was a gay pride parade in Center City that day. I hadn't seen too many drag queens at that point so they were amazing to me. I bought a shirt with a picture of Joan Crawford on it that said WWJD: WHAT WOULD JOAN DO? I filmed us telling Peter what he was missing. Mario scolded me for capturing both of us in the most unflattering angles possible. (In retrospect his enormous nose looks like my mother's. But to me that made him more, not less, gorgeous.)

I have pictures of us at the fountain in Center City next to huge red letters that say LOVE. I have pictures of us outside a bar called Moriarty's and next to a statue. I took pictures of myself in the dressing room at Macy's where Mario went to get himself a tight T-shirt for the club. I asked him why he didn't just wear his tank top, and he said he didn't want to look slutty. When dusk set in, a pink-and-blue sunset reflecting against the marble sculptures that sit at the top of the old bank in Center City, we went back to the parking garage and climbed into Mario's blue Hyundai to change our clothes for the club.

I got out my camera and took a picture of Mario as he smiled at me from the driver's seat in the dim yellow light of the car. In the backseat, I stripped off my shirt and red leather skirt and handed him my camera. A car drove by, and I grabbed a knit blanket to cover myself. He took a picture of me as I lifted the corner to peek out at him.

"Should we plan on sleeping here?" I asked.

"I'll find somewhere for both of us," Mario assured me. "I promise." He held my shoulders and looked into my eyes, and I gazed back into his. He took my hand as we left the parking garage.

"Come on, I'll show you the club I found." We walked over the cobblestones together, and I watched the people start to come out of their houses. Few of them, I thought, looked as pretty as us.

Mario picked up speed, and we started running through the streets of Philadelphia. He led me through the parks and alleyways of Old City, the layers of my Chaiken chiffon dress flapping behind me. It occurred to me that Mario would make a great reality-TV star. His enthusiasm is contagious, and his sharp beauty easy to understand. He giggled as he took a swig of the sticky cherry bourbon he was keeping in a Coke bottle. He handed it to me.

"I don't know if I can hack this, beautiful," I said gently.

Mario grinned, his green eyes crinkling. "The lesbians will buy you all the drinks you want."

We reached a grim-looking alley. Groups of gay guys were standing outside the door, including a chubby guy with curly hair whose shirt said HI. YOU'LL DO. There were a few groups of straight girls, and some lesbians.

"Our stop," he said as he brought me to the door. The bouncer put Xs on our hands and we entered the club.

It was only 10:00, so there weren't that many people. It was a small club, with mirrors on all of the walls and flashing lights. The drinks weren't expensive. I started to lead Mario to the dance floor, but surprisingly he doesn't like to dance unless he's drunk. He moved to the bar and perched on the side in the most unassuming fashion he could muster, his trim figure highlighted with each green, blue or red flash of the lights. I moved over to the mirrors and as the music picked up I circled the floor, matching the rhythm, dancing with myself. My dancing is more earnest than sexy, I've learned, and a group of boyish-looking lesbians were watching me.

"You're so cute!" one of them said. She was a tall, handsome (that's the right word) black woman with an Afro who looked about twenty-eight. "Can I dance with you?"

I tried to follow her moves, but I'm better when I'm dancing fast and alone. She led me to the pool table and bought a game. She was chatty and fun. Her short white girlfriend with long beaded dreadlocks came back with a pitcher of beer. They shared it with me as the black girl beat me in pool. She pinched my cheek and said, "Later baby," as she and her partner walked off.

Mario stumbled to the pool table and breathed a vodka-laden greeting at me. I handed him my camera and tumbled onto the pool table as he took a blurry pink-and-green picture.

"You're beautiful, Mario," I said.

"You're beautiful too," he slurred. "I'm going outside for a bit. I'll be back."

I danced some more, but the club was filling up with people. I wanted to talk to the guy with long blond hair and a sparkling red thong, but the club was getting smaller and louder and there were too many bright colors and people sounded like they were cackling and it gave me a headache. They turned on the smoke and all I could see was dozens of vague figures writhing about in front of all the mirrors. I pushed past their sweaty bodies to the door. I thought I'd get used to sensory overload the more I went to clubs, but I didn't. As I walked out for a breather a skinny girl handed me a cigarette. She cupped her hand around it to help me light up. The awful smell and the steps I had to take to smoke it correctly brought me back to focus.

I trudged along the sidewalk looking for Mario. "Nice dress, bitch!" yelled a guy sitting on the curb. I realized that he thought I was a lesbian, and that "bitch" was a compliment. I smiled back at him, stepping prettily. "Thanks."

Mario was walking with a handsome guy who looked like he was in his midthirties. He had an attractive slouch and moved with a bit of a swagger. He wasn't an especially big guy, but he had a very deep voice. Mario skipped over and introduced us.

"Gwendolyn, this is Leon," he said, slurring a bit, his manners impeccable even if his diction wasn't. He dragged me over to the stairs to chat.

"I told you I'd find somewhere for us to go."

"Us?"

"Hey." Mario put his hand on my shoulder. "If you're nervous, we can just find a motel. I came here with you and I want you to be happy. You're one of my best friends, Gwendolyn." His green eyes were wide and he was the most guileless person I'd ever seen.

"I trust you," I told him. "I'd like to hang out with Leon."

"You can sleep in the room with us. I won't let him kick you out."

I sadly ran my hand along his back. "I know."

Leon loaded us up in his car. We were headed to a motel in Cherry Hill, New Jersey. As hurt as I was that Mario had sullied our time together by soliciting a proposition, my role was to be up for anything.

"That club's a little skeezy," Leon said protectively. "I'm glad we got out of there before it closed."

I looked out the window at the Denny's, Roy Rogers and Exxon signs along the highway to the motel. I took a picture of the road outside the windshield, getting Leon's profile from the back and his short hair. He was an Army lieutenant, and he had lovers in several cities. Mario was awed by his globe-trotting. He struck me as a kind man. He didn't think it was at all strange that Mario brought me with them.

The room was standard-issue Motel 6. I got a few chips from the machine. When I came back, Mario was in the shower. I crawled under the heavy sheets on the king-size bed. But when I turned around, Leon was next to me. I was stunned as he crawled on top of me.

"Wouldn't it be funny," he murmured, "if Mario came back out of the shower and thought we were having sex?"

"Yeah, but you're gay..."

"I've had sex with girls before."

He was still for a moment, and I ran my hand lightly across

his weathered shoulder. He was tending toward premature gray, and I wanted to ask him if he'd been to Afghanistan and what he did there. He kissed the skin below my neck, and moved my mouth up to his. He tasted like Listerine and cigarettes. He felt me furrow my eyebrows and he chuckled softly. "It's all right."

When Mario came out of the shower he saw Leon kissing me, my legs wrapped around his hips. He sat gingerly on the side of the bed. Leon moved up to kiss Mario.

"Are you okay?" he asked. Mario nodded.

"Gwendolyn?" Leon asked.

"Yeah."

"You guys ever done this before?"

Mario and I said no in unison. Leon arranged the three of us so we were sitting in a triangle.

"Have you ever made out?" he asked.

"Once," I said.

Leon watched us kiss. Mario isn't a leader, but kissing him under Leon's authority set the dynamic. But as I ran my hands over my beloved he was more responsive than usual. He cupped my breast and Leon rubbed his shoulders. He moved down Mario's body and unzipped his black jeans. I stared at the base of Mario's penis as Leon sucked him. I ran a finger along Mario's chest as he writhed, proud that I could watch him feel that good. He squeezed his eyes tight and he shook a little bit as he came.

I lay on my back and waited for them to address me. Leon crawled to my side, and he didn't come up. I felt the air moving before he got up to the tops of my thighs and moved in. He was dexterous, his tongue sliding across my clit with command as he drew the tension forward. He knew to lick faster as my thighs and my chest tightened up and he knew to hold my hips down as he brought me to release.

Mario was sitting up with a bemused look on his face. He looked a little bit silly but I pulled him to me. We'd been pleasured together in camaraderie. He let me kiss him again. He let me run my hands and my mouth down his abs, and I licked the remnants of the hickey I'd left there the other time he'd let me make out with him. He let me climb onto him and sheath his long cock with the condom Leon handed to me. I fastened Mario's hips between my legs and lowered onto him, trying to push away all the implications as I rode astride the boy I fruitlessly loved.

He pushed into me from beneath me, but he wasn't an active lover. I ran my hand along the base of his cock to feel my wetness on his skin. It was taking him a while to get into it, but when he saw Leon looking at us with an amused grin on his face he started moving his hands tentatively over my body.

I was determined to wring out every inch of Mario's pleasure. I started moving faster and he started matching my strides, the pressure building as I angled the head of his cock against my front wall. I arched my back and my chest all the way through so my A-spot felt thicker.

Then Leon came up behind me and slipped a wet finger in my ass just a little bit. He put on a condom and pushed me onto Mario's beautiful body, sliding into me from the back. I tightened up and both of them pulled me down against them and pumped me hard. The urgent tightness in the back and the fullness in the front squeezed everything together in three inches of a thousand pounds of pleasure. Both of them slammed like tanks into that tiny space and I screamed as I came from my front and back wall in a much wider orgasm than I'd known I could have before.

I caught my breath as I pulsed afterward. I held Mario as he came, then Leon ran his hands over Mario's shoulders and my sides as he finished. They pulled out. Leon chuckled and Mario squinted at me. My part was over.

When I woke up the bed was moving. I rolled over and saw Mario's legs slung over Leon's shoulders. Leon was pumping into him, and I wasn't as turned off as I thought I'd be by watching the man I wanted being spread wide open like that for another man. It looked like the natural order of things. But I noticed that Mario wasn't a particularly active lover for Leon either. He didn't move much as Leon pumped, and he just lay there dopily as Leon pulled out, not wearing a condom, and came all over his chest. Leon jumped up and went to the shower without looking at me.

"Hey," said Mario, a lazy smile on his beautiful face.

"Hey."

"I feel kind of like a bitch," he confessed.

"Well, you look kind of like one too," I said. He paused for a second. Then we both laughed.

Leon came out of the shower and dressed, then he kissed Mario's head. I smoothed my Chaiken dress. I went in the bathroom to clean up. I looked at myself in the mirror. *This is the face of a girl who just fucked two gay men.* It was the kind of self-conscious exhilaration that only comes with doing something outrageous. Nobody could ever take this experience away from me.

Mario rushed up to me when I came out. He was holding a drawstring plastic bag with the American Eagle Outfitters logo on it.

"Leon had these in his car for me," he said excitedly. "He'd bought them for another guy, but he said I could have them. Isn't that nice?"

"That's pretty cool, new clothes," I said flatly.

"He might not ever see me again and he did that. That was so nice!"

When Leon drove us back to Philly, he got Mario's number. He tactfully kissed him good-bye and gave me a huge hug. Mario and I chatted on the ride home about Peter Salisbury and Cody. We agreed not to tell them what happened, because it wasn't going to change anything at all. He said nothing about the fact that we'd had sex, because it meant nothing to him. He walked me to my room. I kissed his cheek and watched him smile.

ACCIDENTAL TRANSMISSION

Beatrix Ellroy

Sian dropped into her armchair, bowl of ice cream at her elbow, ready for her hot date with her news feed. She flipped her laptop open and nestled her way into the lush fabric of the chair, its arms curving around her. She flicked through her open tabs, then went suddenly still.

The video feed was still up from her chat earlier with Izet. Even though they'd run in the same circles for years, bumping into each other at events and parties, workshops and conferences, this was the first time they'd worked closely together and so far she'd been enjoying it. The banter, the wit, how easy he was on the eyes. They'd been talking about a project they were both freelancing on, and messing about with a bunch of different web apps for video chat.

One of which was still streaming.

He obviously didn't realize he was broadcasting. That he was on her screen. He was still in his chair, headphones around his neck, but he was leaning back, his soft cotton shirt rucked up over the dark hair of his belly. His pants undone and his hand moving under the fabric of his jeans, his underwear.

Sian felt a chill run through her, followed by fire, rippling over her skin. Her nipples hardened beneath her camisole and she spread the fingers of one hand over her chest, the other hovering over her keyboard. Began to breathe silently through her mouth. She knew she should close the window, maybe say something. Not sit here, tensing the muscles of her thighs and running her fingers over her clavicles.

She stayed silent, mouth open, as Izet's head fell back and his hand moved. As he shifted in the seat, one hand pulled his shirt farther up, the dark skin of his stomach made darker by the hair, thick and pelted from his belly button to the still-covered shadow between his legs. She swallowed hard and willed him to move more, do more. The desire to see him, his cock hard and leaking, rose up. She bit her lip, worrying at it, her fingers curving beneath the edge of her cami, stroking the soft skin of her upper breast. Izet shook his head and shifted in his seat again, spreading his legs as wide as the chair would allow. Sian held her breath, waiting. She was rewarded.

He leaned back, shuffling forward to spread his legs wider as he drew his cock from his underwear. His hand, broad and wide, moved against the smooth flesh. Sian felt herself slicken, her muscles inside clench and quiver. His cock was thick, nestled in dark hair, with a vein running along its length. She shut her eyes, breathed through her nose, gathering the remnants of her morals.

"Izet!" she said, but it came out too soft, too weak.

As much as she longed to see his hand move more, harder and faster until he came, as much as her body clenched and twisted at the thought of his face as he lost the barriers between his self and pleasure, in spite of all that, she couldn't do it.

"Izet!" She leaned into her laptop mic as she spoke and typed a quick message in Skype, trusting it would pop up.

Sian: *IZET! You're still streaming.*

Her words, onscreen and through his headphones, broke through Izet's inattention. He looked questioningly at his screen, letting go of his cock to move his mouse. Sian could pinpoint the moment he realized. He winced, and a flush rose up. He moved his hand and the stream shut down. Sian let out a shuddering sigh.

Sian: *Izet, it's okay.*

She waited, one hand on her lips. A few moments later she finally heard the familiar chime.

Izet: *No, it really isn't.*

Sian: *I'm sorry, I didn't mean to perv on you like that—I should have said something earlier.*

Izet: ...

Izet: *What do you mean earlier? How long were you watching?*

Sian: *Long enough to know what you were doing.*

Izet: *How long? And why?*

Sian sighed, put her own headset on and then hit the voice call button. After a painful wait Izet picked up. His voice was rougher than normal, deep and caramel. She swallowed before speaking.

"Hi." She coughed. "Um, yeah, so..."

He laughed, nervously. "Yeah, so. You kept watching?"

"Um. Yes? I'm sorry, I should have said something when I first realized. You know. What you were doing."

She could hear his chair creak as he moved. "Why would you keep watching though?"

"Well. I." She cleared her throat again. "I guess, I liked it."

Izet was silent for a moment. "You liked watching me, ah, touch myself?"

Sian laughed. "Yes, Izet, I liked watching you touch yourself. Why wouldn't I?" She felt arousal curling in the pit of her stomach, making her bold. "Your hand, stroking up along your cock, that patch of hair on your belly? It's a good look."

She heard the rough sound as Izet bumped his mic. "I…"

"Izet?"

"Yes?"

"Turn on the video."

Sian watched as Izet came into view. He waved sheepishly.

"You're not turning yours on?"

"No, not right now. Right now I want you to start again."

He ran one hand over his face, resting it on his cheek over the wiry bristles of his beard. "Start again? You want me to touch myself on camera for you?"

"Yes."

"I want to see you."

"Not yet, Izet, not yet. I want to watch you come first; I want to see you make yourself come for me. Let me see."

Sian watched avidly as Izet shifted while she spoke, rubbed his hands over his thighs. Covered his face before he finally nodded, silent. His hands moved down his chest and across the expanse of his belly. With one hand he pulled up his shirt and the other pressed into his pants.

"What do you think about, Izet?" Sian's voice was low, bourbon-smooth. "Tell me, Izet. Tell me."

Izet's eyes closed and his hand moved more, pulling his shirt up higher, straining the fabric. "Right now? Right now I'm thinking about you." His voice was raw. "About you watching me."

"Telling you what to do?"

"Yes." He hissed out the word and pushed the heel of his hand against his cock and gasped. "Fuck, please?"

"That's it, Izet, I want you to moan, let me hear it." She licked her lips. "Take your cock out, let me see it."

Izet moaned and pushed his underwear down, freeing his cock. Sian could see wetness glistening at the tip, and she swallowed hard. Her clit was begging for attention; she could feel wetness soaking through her underwear.

"Now stroke, root to tip." He did and moaned. "Again."

"Fuck, Sian."

"Shhhh. That's good, honey, once more. Now, get your pants off. Then I want you to hitch your knees up, spread your legs."

He pushed his pants down over his hips, over his ass, to drop on the floor.

"Shirt?" he asked.

"Yeah, that too."

He pulled his shirt up and over, his muscles and shoulders flexing, wrestling and swearing as the cord from his headset got tangled. He settled himself back in the chair, hitched his knees over the arms of his chair, spreading himself, his bare toes curling as his hand moved through the hair on his chest.

"Oh yes," Sian breathed. "Izet, that's great, honey. Fuck." Sian inhaled, heavy and hard. Willing her hand to keep still, to not relieve the ache between her thighs. "Now, touch yourself like you normally would. Show me."

Izet's hand moved from his chest to his throat and the other curled around his cock, stroking it from root to tip, firm and unrelenting. His toes curled and uncurled and his free hand clutched up near his throat moved down to cup his balls, almost like he was weighing them, his thumb stroking down the rapidly tightening flesh.

Sian breathed heavily, squeezing her thighs together.

"I want you to slow it down." She leaned forward. "Spread your legs wider. I want to see you better."

She watched as he bit his lip and did as she asked; after a moment he stopped and leaned forward himself, adjusting his webcam.

"Is that better?"

Most of her screen was taken up by him now, framing his cock. But his face was just off the screen.

"I want to see your face."

He moved the webcam slightly, then smiled into it. "How about now?"

"Oh yes, that's perfect." She sighed and licked her lips. "Now, like I said, slow it down, let me see."

He moved his hand slower, spreading his thighs wider, stroking his fingers along the crease of his thigh, the seam of his balls.

"Yes, that's it, farther down sweetheart. I just want you to press against the flesh behind your balls. Not your ass, just that bit of flesh."

He opened his eyes like he was staring at her, then closed them again, letting his head fall back. One hand kept slowly moving along his cock and the other crept back, curving and cupping his balls before dipping farther behind, disappearing into the shadows. The hand on his cock stuttered again, then sped up.

Sian shook her head. "Ah, I said slowly. Take your hand off your cock."

Izet's eyes flew open, and he glared at the webcam.

"Izet, take your hand off your cock." Sian let a hint of steel infuse her voice and felt a thrill run through her when he put his hands on his thighs. "Just your cock, honey, keep your other hand down there, keep it busy."

Izet whined but did as he was told and his hand dipped back down, moving against his perineum.

"Do what you want there, whatever feels good. But leave your cock alone."

He nodded and she could see his wrist flex and move, his fingers hidden. His brows were drawn together and his mouth open, his tongue darting out to lick his lips every few moments.

"Tell me, how does it feel? How do you feel?"

Izet shifted in his seat, squirming, and Sian felt a thrill of joy. "Christ. Not enough, it's just not enough," he hissed. "God, I want to touch my cock, I want to touch you."

"Be good and you might just get to."

He moaned, low and soft, and his hips flexed. Sian felt her own hips move in sympathy.

"Fuck, Sian, please? I want to..." He moaned. "I want to touch my cock, I want to come for you, please?"

Sian couldn't help it and her own hand moved between her thighs, beneath her underwear, dipping into the slickness and circling her clit.

"Oh god, Izet, you are so fucking lovely. Touch yourself, touch your cock."

His hand moved, one still nestled in the shadows, the other gripping and stroking, twisting up at the end of the stroke to curl around the glistening head of his cock. She moaned, sudden and wanton, and Izet's hand flexed hard.

"Sian, I'm going to come." His hand moved faster.

"Fuck yes, Izet, come for me, I want to see it." Her own fingers moved, dipping inside then rubbing down firmly on her clit. "Do it, come, now." Her voice cracked slightly, and she barely held back her own whimper as Izet curled forward.

"No, open your eyes; look at me when you come."

Izet whimpered and looked up, teeth bared. "I want to see you."

Sian's free hand moved, turning her own feed on. She leaned into the mic and brought her glistening fingers up to the camera. "Watch me, Izet, watch me and come."

She buried her hand back between her legs and worked her clit furiously, her eyes locked on the screen, watching Izet bite his lip, twist his hand and finally come, staring through the camera as his cock jerked and spasmed. After a moment he brought his hand, coated with come, up to the camera.

His tongue darted out and licked a stripe through the wetness and Sian whimpered and then came herself, hips jerking upward. She breathed out a moan, pulling her hand free and bringing it up to her own camera, even as she clenched through the aftershocks.

For a moment they sat still, watching each other on the screen. The silence lengthened and threatened to become awkward until Sian started giggling; Izet smiled and raised an eyebrow.

"Well, I should go and shower." He raised one hand and ruefully wiggled it at her. She snickered, then looked mournfully at the bowl next to her.

"And my ice cream has melted." Izet laughed and she mockglowered at him. "I wasn't expecting to get so...distracted."

"Well, you did. Thoroughly."

"I'm not going to use that particular service again, and I'll submit a bug report. But I'll be better prepared next time."

"Next time?"

She looked down. "If you want to, that is."

He leaned into the camera again. "I was hoping next time would be a little more interactive, that's all."

"I'd definitely need to be more prepared in that case."

"Well, let's say we try for Friday night?"

Sian smiled. "Sounds good to me." She kissed the tips of

her fingers and waved them at the camera and Izet smiled in response before signing off. Sian blinked a few times before getting up and dumping the melted ice cream into the sink and heading for her bedroom, and her bedside table. The ache had barely subsided, and the promise of Friday night was still too far away.

She couldn't wait.

GROPED

Lana Fox

There I was, on the Boston subway at rush hour, dressed in a tight, white, partly unbuttoned blouse, with a short pleated skirt and socks that rose over my knees. Schoolgirl material. I stood by the doors, holding on while the train sped toward Park Street, and the young guy in earbuds, who was standing just to my left, glanced down the front of my blouse.

Do it! I told him with my eyes, arching my body toward his. I was so close that he could easily brush his arm or leg against my own, and my blood was pumping for it—I could hear it in my ears. Christ, I was practically rubbing my pussy against him, all hot and wet and ready. And for a moment, he looked right at me and I saw the lust in those heavy brown eyes.

Grope me, you asshole! Put a hand on my tits! Stick one under my skirt! And I waited, edging closer, to feel his fingers touch my thigh, and hear his groan of pleasure when he found I was wearing no underwear. I waited, wet as hell, just hoping I'd found a pervert to stick his fingers into my cunt and fuck me in front of the world.

It had started six months ago because of a gorgeous porn flick. Not long after my boyfriend had moved out, I was watching an anime cartoon about a woman who longed to be fucked on the subway. She tried to get groped several times, but just before a guy would be ready to stick his hands on her, she'd always lose her nerve and edge away. At last, she gave in to an older guy who rubbed his hands all over her body and eventually fucked her in full view of everyone.

But that wasn't the hottest moment for me. No, the high point came when he stuck his hands up her skirt and stroked her buttocks, followed by her pussy. It was the pervy act of being groped by a bastard—that's what gave me the best climax I'd ever had.

In the weeks after I saw that movie, I'd climaxed over and over, every single day. I was desperate to get touched up whenever I took the subway, and had pushed my ass into dozens of thirsty faces. Yes, I'd been so turned on, waiting for some sweet sucker to fondle my ass and pussy in public. I could even have humped a stranger's knee—that's how wet I was. But there's a limit. I mean, you can't force others into stuff like that, right? Besides, the best grope was the quiet grope, the sly hands cupping my warm buttocks, the shape of a cock pressing against my crack. Hell, if someone would do it, I'd come like a fucking steam train.

I just needed some gorgeous pervert to take the bait.

But even while I was standing close to the guy in the earbuds, feeling his stare on my body like a laser, watching him bite his lips—even when I turned so my buttocks were there, begging his hands for some serious dirt, I knew he was just going to walk away and fantasize about me later. Christ, what was wrong with the men in this town? Why couldn't I just get groped?

"Sweetie, you're mad," said my friend Barney the following night at the pub. He was wearing a peaked cap today—a fawn-brown number that matched his eyes. "I mean, what if someone gets rough with you? You can't just hand yourself to anyone."

I told him I could do what I liked, thank you very much, but he looked concerned. Barney is usually such a mischief-maker, that when he gets serious, you have to worry. "Barns, brighten up! I'll be careful, okay?"

He gave a shrug and downed a few gulps of Guinness. "I mean, they're obviously loopy," he said, as he placed down the glass. "If I was straight, flower, I'd grope your little ass off." He giggled, then he lowered his eyes. When he looked back up, they were soft with feeling. "But sweetie, any trouble, just call me, all right? I love your feistiness, but I worry."

God bless my Barns. I gave him a big, warm smile. "Sure," I said, "but I'll snag my fish soon enough." Then I recrossed my legs beneath the table where just the thought of being groped by a stranger was making me horny again.

After a beat, Barn's eyebrows shot up—I'd seen that look in meetings, when a marketing idea struck him. "Hey," he said at last, with that classic, puppy-dog smile. "Why not pay someone to grope you? It'd be their best score yet."

"Maybe," I mused, but it just wasn't the fantasy. I wanted it to be pervy, not the fulfillment of a request.

"Okay, I get it," he sighed. Then he leaned in closer and said, "But I see the prob. They'd grope your ass off, if they knew." He snickered. "Maybe we'll get you a T-shirt that says, I'M BEGGING FOR A FUMBLE."

"I mean, I'm practically waving my cunt in their faces!"

"They don't want to push," said Barns. "And let's face it, that's impressive."

I nodded and gave a sigh. As usual, Barns was right. "I guess

I'll have to actually ask someone to do it," I said, "but that defeats the whole fantasy...."

"Wait a flea-picking minute!" said Barney, bobbing a finger in my direction. "I've got an idea...."

It was a good idea, Barney's idea. He had a friend who was kinky. Would I be interested in a role-play or two? But I soon managed to convince myself that it wouldn't be the same. So I returned to my nightly attempts on the subway. Recently, I'd been keeping to rush hour, trying to take advantage of the crowds. I figured it was easier to grope a woman when you were slammed together like sardines. But what if I pushed things later? It seemed a little more dangerous to wear a short skirt on a late-night train, but a drink or two loosens folks up, and I was getting so desperate for some wandering hands that I'd been dressing up at home, putting on a silky evening glove and fondling my own damn ass.

Actually, it had been getting me off so beautifully that I'd started taking the gloves to work. Just picture it—me, groping my ass in a ladies' room cubicle, coming against the wall of the stall again and again and again. God knows what others thought of my staggered gasps when they entered the restroom. But I didn't care. I was too obsessed. I'd imagine a stranger's hands and I'd feel them on me, and my body would respond with howling joy.

But these lunchtime escapades always left me hungrier. They made me crave the real, perverted thing.

So a few nights later, I'd perfected an outfit: a black velvet dress with a studded collar, high-heeled boots, and stockings with garters. The dress showed enough cleavage to lead anyone on, and it was lined with silky material that felt gorgeous against my bare skin. It was as if my dress itself was the pervert, all insidious and teasing, touching my thighs and buttocks, groping my nipples when I moved. Standing on that train at night with the dress pawing at me, and the train's vibrations purring into me, was enough to push me to the brink.

For a while, it was the same old story—some guy would see me and feast his eyes, until I moved closer, then he'd turn away or look awkward. Then, at Central Square, a man in a suit entered the coach. I was standing by the door, holding on to the bar, and he joined me, up close, with a stalker's stare. His eyes were a startling shade of blue—so bright, in fact, that I had to look away first. He was wearing trendy glasses. And I like men in glasses. "Hi," he said. "Did I die and go to heaven?"

I laughed. My heart started thumping. "Maybe," I said, coyly. That's when he arched in closer.

He glanced down my front. "Oh yes," he said, through a ready sigh. "*Heaven*, that's what you are." I could feel his breath hot on my throat. I was so horny that my mouth was watering. He said, "You're on your way to meet a lover, of course." He laid his fingers on my arm and I felt a volt of pleasure.

Christ, I all but thrust my cunt into his hands.

It happened magically, before I'd even thought to check how many people were sitting in our wake. Watching me with a steady stare, he slid his hand down my side, then over the curve of my hip, and I was a mess of wanting, all trembling and ready, as I felt his hand stroking my dress, pressing the lining onto my body. He put his lips close to my ear and I could smell his aftershave and the warmth of his body beneath it. "Turn around," he said, softly, "so I can see the back of your dress."

I did what he asked in a heartbeat, the lining stroking my nipples as I moved, and immediately, I felt him reach around me and cup my breast. I moaned out loud, desperate for more, pressing right into his touch. He groaned too and that's when

I felt his fingers glossing my buttocks through the velvet dress. Before I knew it, he was telling me to lean forward. There I was, with my hands against the train doors, my ass sticking out as he reached inside my skirt and stroked my cheeks and the tops of my thighs.

I gave a little cry when I felt his cock against me. It was the hardest cock I'd ever felt.

"Fuck, yes," I said. "Do it!" Then I felt his fingers glossing my shaved pussy before pushing right into my cunt. I cried out with pleasure, forgetting where I was, forgetting anyone who might be nearby, because I was just a body, a body in perfect pleasure, a body crying out to be exactly who she was. My lover shuddered, grinding his cock against me, his breathing hard and fast, the tips of his fingers fucking me more quickly— and it took just a few moments of this heavenly torture before he moved away and I heard him unzip. I heard the sounds of a condom being unwrapped, so I stuck my ass out farther, waving it at him, pleading with him—because Jesus, this was as hot as it got and my pussy was all but screaming for more. And when I felt his whole cock filling me, I came straight away, crying out. But that wasn't all. The more he fucked me, the more I came, over and over in quick succession, and when he pushed a hand inside the front of my dress, grasping my breast and saying, "Fuck, I'm gonna come," he hammered that cock into me so damn deep that I wailed out the biggest climax yet—the kind of coming that makes you scared because you've never known power like that.

Just as I was coming down from the high, and I could feel him behind me, sorting himself out, there was an announcement—we were arriving at Porter Square. Suddenly I felt desperately embarrassed. (What had I just done, in front of a whole damn crowd?) Red faced, I pulled down my dress and neatened myself a little, as the train pulled into the station.

Suddenly, I felt him grasp my wrist.

I whirled around to face him. "What are you doing?"

"You're coming with me," he said, with a sideways smile. "I'm going to fuck you to the other side of heaven."

I laughed. "You just *did*." Then I added, "But I have places to be."

"No," he said, his eyes hard on mine. "You're coming with me."

"I'm not," I said, pulling from his grip. "We're done. It was great, but we're done here."

I glanced down the coach, looking for a witness, but holy crap, there was no one there.

"What *are* you?" he said, as the train rolled into the station. "A tease?"

"Sure," I said, angry now. "A tease with *rights*."

"You need me," he said. The train was stopping now, and I couldn't see anyone standing on the platform. "I've never felt a woman come so hard," he said, grasping my arm again. "You want to be dommed and dirtied up. You need me. Let's go."

"I said *no!*" The force of my voice surprised me. So I shouted it again: "No, no, no! I am not going with you—and you can't make me."

The train doors slid open. He tried to grab me again, but I moved away, pulse beating in my ears. He looked like he was going to grasp me again, and that's when I kicked him right in the shin. He jumped at that. "Get off the train!" I shouted. "Or I'll yell and I won't stop."

He paused for a moment, his eyes bright with madness, a sneer of contempt on his face. He looked like he wanted to shove my head down a toilet. But I held his stare, and I stood my ground. Finally, as the doors beeped—a sign that they were closing—he turned and stepped from the coach, without saying another word.

It's strange when the hottest thing that has happened to you suddenly turns gross. And when Barney and I met at the pub that week and I spilled the whole story, I admit my eyes got a little damp. Was my fantasy something I couldn't play out safely? But once I'd let him wipe my eyes with a tissue and had taken a few slugs of beer, I started to feel better. "Tell me straight," I said, (which made us both giggle, because if there's anything Barney is not, it's *straight*). "Was that my fault?" I asked. "I mean, if I'm going to have sex in public, is that what I should expect?"

He squeezed my hand and said, "Don't think it, even for a second. When someone is abusive, it's *their* fault. Not yours."

I lowered my eyes and thought about what he'd said. "If I did do it again," I said, "I'd try to be more subtle...."

"Flower, listen to me! It wasn't your fault. That asshole attacked you! We seriously need to report him."

I thought about all this. Just for a while. The night on the train had been amazingly hot. And it was strange to admit that I'd *found* myself in those moments. Now that I'd played out my fantasy, I knew I wasn't done with it.

"So here's an idea," said Barney. "What if you could do it again with more control? Remember that guy I mentioned? Luke?"

I gazed at him, puzzled for a moment. Then I remembered what he'd suggested the other night—being groped and screwed in public, but by one of his kinky friends. "I suppose it's worth a shot," I said.

Barney's eyes sparkled so much that I smiled. Matchmaking makes him look like a benevolent leprechaun. "You won't be disappointed," he said. "Luke's wild in the sack! He's got a great imagination. You'll love him."

I spoke to Barney's friend Luke on the phone before I met him. It was odd telling a stranger my fantasies about getting off in public, but I admit, it really turned me on. What's more, he was kind and understanding—and he had one helluva sultry voice. "Your fantasy's gorgeous," he told me. "It's something I've always wanted to try, but none of my lovers have ever wanted to go through with it." He told me I was deliciously kinky, and I thanked him, because it sounded like a compliment. Then we set up a liaison that I'd never forget.

We worked it out in a fail-safe way because Luke knew that subway. He knew that if I got on at Central Square from a certain point on the platform, we'd find each other easily. Sure enough, when I got on dressed in a scarlet skirt, carrying an umbrella on a summer's night, I immediately saw a man that matched his description. He was wearing tinted glasses and a Nirvana T-shirt, just as he'd promised, and was reading a copy of *Rolling Stone*—just as we'd planned.

He was just as gorgeous as Barns had promised—floppy brown hair that tumbled over his soft blue eyes, not to mention a well-built body beneath that tight tee. I sat down next to him, all tense and aroused, and read from my own book, again just as we'd planned. I was ridiculously horny with those stockings casing my legs and a pair of satin panties clutching my ready pussy. *Touch me*, I told him in my head. *Touch me. Please?* But I'd promised we wouldn't talk. He liked the idea of silence.

A couple of minutes in, I wondered if I'd been mistaken because he hadn't so much as looked at me. He was casually turning the pages of his magazine, driving me mad with the smell of his skin and the way he bit his lip as he read. His hair was short at the back and he had a tanned neck that I wanted to bite and kiss. His arms were gorgeous too—toned, but not too muscly.

I pulled my skirt up a little to reveal the lace tops of my stockings and rubbed my aching thighs. It felt so good to be exposing myself like this, with the train's vibrations caressing my pussy, and the tight strappy top clasping my breasts and nipples. I parted my knees, showing him my garters.

But still, he didn't look.

My heart was pumping. I knew what I wanted to do, but what if I was wrong, and this wasn't actually Luke? No! He was simply playing a game, because it had to be him—he was simply playing the game and driving me crazy. And dear god, did I love him for it. So I smiled, wrenched my skirt right up my thighs and touched my pussy through the silky panties.

It felt so good that I gasped, falling back in my seat. That's when I felt his leg pressing against my own. He'd dropped his mag to the floor and stared down at my dirty, groping fingers.

"Fuck," he whispered, "you're perfect."

As our eyes met, I thought I might die with need. Then I felt his fingers replacing my own, felt his fingertips against my sex, felt my clit begging for more. "Oh god," I sighed, "don't stop."

He brought his lips right close to my ear, so I was bathed in his aftershave. "Baby," he whispered, "I'll keep on going as long as you want, as deep as you can take it." With that, he pushed his fingers inside my panties and stroked my wet clit, with a perfect sultry motion, whispering about all kinds of things that he wanted to do—to fuck me against a wall, to lick me under a restaurant table, to tease my nipples with the tip of his tongue as we stood in a room full of artsy sculptures. "I'll touch you everywhere," he told me, "wherever you want. And I'll love every moment of your perfect cunt." With that, I came, sailing into oblivion, taken by a pleasure that pulsed ever deeper. And even though we'd hardly said a word to each other, a part of me knew, even then, we were a match made in heaven.

And you know, I wasn't wrong. Because, to this day, we are.

POSTCARDS FROM PARIS

Giselle Renarde

Emily's heart raced. From the moment Yannik walked in, she couldn't sit still.

"Go ahead," Hunter said with a smirk. "Give the guy a hug."

Emily raced across the restaurant and wrapped her arms around Yannik's neck. "You're here!" She knocked off his top hat when she reached up to kiss his cheek. "Oops, sorry."

"You look lovely," Yannik said, as Emily picked up his hat. "That velvet's a great color."

"Got it at the consignment shop." She handed Yannik his hat and then gave a twirl. "How about *you*? You look very dapper in your tails."

"Why thank you," he said, with a debonair bow.

Emily couldn't get over how good it was to have Yannik back in town. She and Hunter had missed him so much while he was in France. The house wasn't the same with just the two of them.

"Would you lovebirds get over here?" Hunter called from

the table. "Come keep me company. I'm getting lonely all by myself."

Emily led Yannik to the table by the window. Before taking his seat, he kissed Hunter firmly on the mouth. Other patrons took notice, and that used to make Emily uncomfortable. Now it made her unabashedly proud.

"How did it go at the airport?" Hunter asked.

"Same old, same old." Yannik set his hat on the extra chair and picked up a menu. "They took me into one of those little rooms to question me about the packer."

"Did they make you take your pants off?" Emily asked.

"No, thank god. The gal who came to interview me was really apologetic that I got targeted. She said they've all been trained in screening transpeople, and some of her colleagues are just assholes."

Emily laughed. "She actually said that?"

Yannik nodded.

"Fuck, it's just a fake cock," Hunter said. "I don't know why they get so worked up."

The waiter cleared his throat. "Are we were ready to order?"

Emily bit her lip and tried not to grin as the boys ordered dinner. She knew how funny the three of them looked—the men divinely overdressed in vintage tuxedos, she wearing a gown from the twenties and a peacock feather in her hair.

"So, what did you bring us?" Emily asked when the waiter was gone. "I've been looking forward to some fancy French souvenirs."

"Yes, yes," Hunter chimed in. "Perhaps some fine lingerie for the lady?"

Smirking, Yannik reached into his breast pocket. "Postcards from Paris!"

"Postcards?" Emily said. "That's it?"

"These ones are special." Yannik spread them across the table. "They're roughly turn-of-the-century."

Emily glanced around the dining room to make sure nobody else could see. The postcards were very naughty: saucy ladies, naked or half-dressed, lesbian spankings and threesomes...

"Would you look at this one!" Hunter pointed to a nude with a particularly full bush. "You don't see that anymore."

"No indeed," Yannik agreed. "They're all like that, to some degree. A nice natural bush on a nude marked the photograph as erotic."

"Really?" Emily picked up the card Hunter had been drawn to. How could anyone be so hairy?

"Well, think about Old Master paintings," Yannik said. "You don't see pubic hair in classical art pieces. Pussies are kind of...*whitewashed*, I guess. The big, full bushes set these postcards apart from high art. A hairy pussy was meant to titillate."

Emily cringed at the thought of having that much hair inside her panties. "I don't know about that. I like a shaved pussy."

"Yes, we've noticed," Yannik said, looking at Hunter as though they were conspiring in some way. "I think we'd both like to see you...au naturel."

The waiter came by to fill their water glasses and Emily blushed like he could see through her clothes. The boys didn't seem ashamed in the least. They didn't even pack up the postcards.

When the waiter went away, Emily asked, "You're going to take away my razor, aren't you?"

"The moment we get home," Hunter said as Yannik kissed her cheek.

* * *

It was unbearably itchy, growing in. Emily squirmed all day for the first few weeks. Every time she showered, she plotted to steal Hunter's razor out of the medicine cabinet. This wasn't fair. She was uncomfortable all day, and why? Because the boys decreed it.

But Emily could never bring herself to shave. She knew how disappointed they'd be if she went against their word. The punishment would be a moratorium on discipline, and she couldn't bear it. She couldn't go a day without their loving straps or spankings.

Ultimately, Emily was glad she held out. After a couple weeks, her crotch stopped itching so much. A month later, she'd cultivated a respectable bush. The boys took note. They got out a ruler and measured the length. They compared her with the women in the postcards. After a good two months of growing it out, Emily was really rather pleased with herself.

The boys were pleased, too.

"I've never seen this much hair on a woman," Yannik said, in that dark voice that made Emily shiver.

Hunter helped him tie her wrists to her legs, spread-eagled on the couch. Her thighs trembled. She thought she couldn't hold the pose, at first. And then, as other things distracted her, the ache subsided.

"It's dark," Hunter said. "I'm surprised. I thought it would be closer to your hair color, but it's almost black, isn't it?"

"Almost," Emily said, wincing. They always did this—ignored her pain, pretended she was perfectly at ease in whatever position they picked. Didn't matter that her muscles were twitching, stretching, crying out in pain. That's what they wanted.

"Look how wet she is," Yannik said, patting her pussy.

"How can you tell?" Hunter asked. "I can't see a thing beyond that fucking hair."

All Emily could think was, *Don't act so disgusted by my body. You made me do this!* But she bit her lip. She didn't speak.

"There's so much of it." Yannik traced his fingers through her bush, making it stick up like a Mohawk so she looked ridiculous.

They played with her pussy like it was a toy. She wanted to feel embarrassed about all that goddamn hair, but she also loved the attention. Two men, four eyes, ten fingers focused on her hairy little cunt. But the boys' humiliation plot was sagging just a touch, because she *liked* it.

"You're right," Hunter said, shoving one finger up her snatch. "Wow, she *is* wet."

Of course I'm wet! You put on my black stay-up stockings, you split me open, tie my wrists to my legs and start teasing me? How could I not be wet?

"Take your finger out," Yannik said to Hunter. "I want to do something."

The moment Hunter withdrew his finger from Emily's cunt, Yannik spanked it. He smacked her pussy with three fingers, hard enough for a wet echo to ring through the living room. There was nothing she could do to resist. She couldn't move. Her muscles ached, but she remained in the wide-open position they'd chosen for her.

"I love that sound," Hunter said. "Spank her pussy again."

Yannik smacked her without delay, just barely catching her flesh. Her hair acted as a buffer, which was such a tease.

"Again," Hunter encouraged. "Harder."

The next blow warmed her cunt enough that she wondered if her skin was getting red down there. Impossible to see.

"Open her pussy for me," Yannik said. "I want to see the pink."

Hunter growled as he grabbed Emily's lips and parted them

roughly. No, that wasn't good enough—not for Hunter. He clutched her pussy hair and pulled, sending shocks through her body. If she arched forward, she could just make out the deep pink of her wet flesh. Hunter was mostly blocking her view, and he was also pulling on her bush so hard her vision started to blur.

"Watch your fingers," Yannik said to Hunter before spanking Emily's clit.

The first blow was off. It fell to the side. He tried again, and clipped her clit sharply this time. An electric pulse shot through her body. She arched forward, but there was nowhere to go without folding herself into a pretzel.

"That hurt, did it?" Hunter asked.

Emily bit her lip, nodding.

"Yannik." The boys made eye contact, and Hunter commanded, "Do it again."

Another sharp slap met her bare pussy, and she threw herself back against the couch. Her thighs screamed for a second, then got warm. Her pussy was glowing when he hit it again, catching her clit off guard. Her ass tightened up as a burst of lightning surged through her arms. Her heart raced. All of her body was connected to her clit—spank it and everything reacted.

Yannik offered a steady stream of spankings. "I wonder how long I can do this before she starts to cry."

Ahh, the power of suggestion...

Either Yannik's blows were falling harder, or Emily's flesh had been as tenderized as she could handle. Tears welled in her eyes. She bit her lip hard to keep quiet.

"Use something else besides your hand," Hunter said, egging Yannik on. They always played this way—boys against girl, plotting every way to torture her. "Get the crop. That'll work perfect."

"Ooh, yeah." Yannik jumped up and raced to the spare room, where all their sexual paraphernalia was kept.

Hunter had been staring at her pussy all this time, but he looked into her eyes now. Something about the angular line of his jaw made her heart beat a little faster, especially when he smiled in that conniving way of his. Emily blinked, and her tears fell in searing streaks down her cheeks.

"I don't think we're ever going to let you shave again," Hunter said, pressing two fingers inside her swollen cunt. Two, then three. Emily whimpered when he rubbed that spot inside— the G-spot so many people claimed didn't exist. Well, something was in there, and Hunter had no problem finding it. She whimpered as he stroked her.

"Uh-oh," Yannik said, standing behind Hunter with his unassuming black crop. "Looks like someone's enjoying herself a little too much."

Hunter grinned. "Wouldn't want that. Emily's already spoiled, living with two hot guys."

"Guys who buy her vintage gowns and take her to fancy dinners," Yannik replied. "Emily's the most spoiled little girl I've ever met."

"Same here," Hunter said, as he fucked her with his fingers. "We give her everything she needs and all she does is take, take, take."

"Greedy, greedy girl." Yannik whisked Hunter's fingers out of the way and loomed between her legs. "Greedy girl deserves a smack."

She'd been smacked a good many times already, by Yannik's own hand, but she wouldn't remind him. Emily knew how to behave. She could keep her mouth shut with the best of them.

Yannik slid the small tongue of his crop between her spread legs. Emily could feel her slick wetness coating the black leather as he drew it up to her clit, then back down again. Her pussy was sopping, dripping juice along her asscrack. She missed being able to see what was going on down there, that gorgeous leather sliding against her bare flesh, but the longer she grew out her bush, the more affection she felt for it—like a crop she'd cultivated herself, and could take pride in. There sure was a lot of hair.

"I hope you're ready for this," Yannik said, and brought the crop down hard.

Emily cringed even before the leather tongue touched her. The desperate cry it made as it whipped through the air was more than enough to send the fear of god through her body. She tried to close her legs, but her bindings made it too difficult. All she could manage was to roll so the crop caught her hairy pussy rather than her glistening, cherry-red clit.

"Oh, Em, that was not smart." Yannik stood back for a moment. "If you can't be trusted to keep still, you know what's in store."

She stared at him, no response. Her heart clambered into her throat. It was all she could hear as Hunter climbed onto the couch. Facing away from her, he straddled her body, and held her legs open by the ankles. Once he'd found a good position, he set his weight on her so she couldn't struggle. All she could see now was the back of his T-shirt. All she could feel was his grip around her ankles. His fingers were still wet with her juice.

"Hold her good and still." Yannik traced that little leather tongue up and down Emily's splayed pussy. It was such a tease, not being able to see. The suspense was torture enough.

And then Yannik slapped her clit with the crop, and she screamed bloody murder because, god, it hurt. It hurt like hell. Her tender pussy blazed, sending explosions right through her nervous system. The pain was so severe she thought about using her safeword. She thought about it, but...Christ, she wanted more. She did.

Hunter gripped her ankles a little harder as Yannik whipped her pussy—twice, this time, in rapid succession. The first one didn't even register until the second strike hit. Then, her hips bucked without her consent, and Hunter sat heavier on her belly, molding her body around his, and driving her back into the soft couch cushions, for which she was thankful.

She didn't realize she was mumbling until Yannik hushed her. What had she been saying? *It hurts. It hurts. I can't stand it. It hurts so much...*

Yannik struck her again, and she wished to god she could see her clit. It felt utterly distended, as big as a cherry. Did it look that way, or were her nerve endings blowing things out of proportion?

Between strikes, her pussy seemed to absorb all the cool air in the room. Her clit was blazing. It hurt. Why did she want more of this? She must be crazy.

"Do it again," Hunter encouraged. "I love the way she shakes when you hit her clit. Her whole body trembles."

"Does it?" Yannik brought the crop down on her pussy. This time, instead of just smacking her clit and moving the leather tongue away, he left it there, pressing squarely against her clit.

"It burns!" she screamed. Emily always tried to keep quiet while the boys were working her over, but she couldn't manage that now. Her body was blazing, like her pussy had caught fire. "Fuck, it hurts! It burns!"

"Really?" Yannik asked, slapping her again, with that same callous trick of leaving the crop flush to her clit. "It burns?"

"Yes!" Emily was crying, sobbing. They obviously couldn't see her face, but couldn't they hear it in her voice? "Guys, it's killing me. It hurts so much!"

"This does?" *Smack.* "This hurts?" *Smack.* "A lot?" *Smack.*

"I can't take it anymore!" Tears coursed down her cheeks as Hunter pressed his back against her face. His spine dug into her cheek, but that was the least of her concerns. "It hurts so fucking much!"

"It hurts, huh?" Yannik smacked her dispassionately, like he was doling out a predetermined punishment. Every strike was measured, metronomic. He played her body like an instrument. Every blow made her sing.

"It hurts," she sobbed into Hunter's back. His shirt absorbed the mess as her nose ran and her tears flowed. She was even drooling on him, because she couldn't manage to close her mouth between sobs. Her words weren't words anymore, just a steady stream of, "Ahhh."

"Think she's had enough?" Yannik asked Hunter. He traced the leather tongue around the perimeter of her pussy, like he was mowing her pubic hair from the outside in. "Maybe she's forgotten her safeword."

"Has Emily forgotten her safeword password?" Hunter asked, loosening his grip on her ankles.

"No." Emily wiped her face across Hunter's back. "I didn't forget."

"Well," Yannik said solemnly. "Sometimes daddies know best."

Hunter bowed to her pussy and spit. That soft drizzle landed like a balm against her clit, soothing her blazing flesh. Part of her wanted more from the crop. It hurt like fuck, but crying was cathartic. She loved sobbing wildly while her men destroyed her. But she trusted them above all else. If they said she'd had enough, she'd had enough.

Yannik untied her wrists, but warned, "I wouldn't close your legs, if I were you."

When Hunter rose from on top of her, Emily got her first glimpse at her hot, red pussy. It looked even more engorged than it felt. She must be seeing things wrong. How could her little pussy possibly look so distended? So fat and red and ripe?

"Sit still and relax," Hunter said. He left the room while Yannik turned on the radio, and reappeared with a damp cloth. When he set it against her blazing cunt, she let out a sigh because nothing had ever felt so good.

Emily sat with her legs wide open, and Yannik settled on the floor between them, kissing her thighs while Hunter sang along with the radio.

"Hey, is there something on my back?" he asked Emily, sitting beside her on the couch. "My shirt feels all wet."

"I don't know, man." She bit her lip to keep from snickering. "Maybe you were sweating a lot."

Yannik shook his head. He knew her too well. "How's your pussy feeling?"

"Still hurts," she said as Hunter adjusted the cloth against her mound. "You know what's weird? I'm really starting to like all this hair."

"I had a feeling you would." Yannik glanced at the wall above the couch, where he'd hung his postcards from Paris. "Growing a full bush is a lost art, but the impact is just as erotic in person as it was in those photographs, if you ask me."

"Me too," Hunter replied, looking up at the postcards.

Emily couldn't see the cards from where she was sitting. Instead, she gazed between her legs, into the dark bush she'd cultivated out of nothing. With a smile, she said, "Me three."

MAGIC TRICKS

Sue Lenèe Cix

I'm busy doing a whole lot of nothing when I hear Danny's step in the hall. The creaky door swings open, and there's rustling: the sound of his raincoat coming off. "Hi, beau," I call.

"Hi," he says, walking in, his shoulders swung back and his head lilted to the side. Silvery moisture clings to his hair; his eyelashes are damp. He's got a white bag in his hand—the kind that gifts come in. He looks proud of something. "How's the search?" he says, flashing movie-star teeth.

"Mournful," I say, pouting. I half-close the laptop I've been staring at, supposedly seeking jobs. "What's in the bag?" I ask.

He winks. "A little something I picked up today. I gotta go to work. I just wanted to bring this over." He shifts from one foot to the other, rests a hand on my shoulder. Something sturdy and clear seeps from his skin to mine, and I breathe him in: cardamom, clove, mahogany, nightfall, magic. He unfurls my fingers to put the handle of the bag there, kisses the ridge of muscle between my shoulder and neck and then hurries out the door.

I wait for the click of the handle, touching where he touched, savoring. I feel his gorgeous presence dissipate from the room, and I close my eyes, relishing the space between contact and desire. Knowing Danny, I suspect that the contents of this bag might have more to offer me than the Job Search page of the Council of Nonprofits website.

So I go ahead and reach in. My hand closes around a tall plastic tube. I lift it out, and start laughing. Inside the tube is: a dick. Dark green, it waits inside a transparent sheath, looking a little like some prop for an absurdist sci-fi movie. It's high quality, good silicone, erected from a little round base of the same color and consistency. The package slides open, and I take the thing in my hand. It wags at me, pert. I close a fist around it, feel it yield slightly to my grip. The tip swells outward in a pleasing likeness to Danny's.

The bag still feels heavy, so I stick my hand back in and retrieve a small package containing coiled leather straps, situated around a cool steel ring.

Oh boy.

My cunt stirs. Danny and I talked about this, not so many weeks ago. We were lying in bed, too tired to fuck, but wandering in and out of each other's fantasies, trying to find new things to learn about each other. I was explaining what kind of boobs I like—which, truly, is most of them, but particularly ones with pointy nipples. Danny said, "Do you ever fantasize about having a dick?"

I laughed, overwhelmed. Danny's sexiness is blunt, open faced, shameless. He's teaching me. But still, I stumbled, unsure what to say. What person hasn't fantasized alternate sexual organs? Sometimes when I'm fucking, two fingers shoving hard against my G-spot, I can almost feel my clitoris swelling into a hungry column, so hard it could enter something.

He waited for my silence to become speech. "Who doesn't?"
I said, remaining offhanded, sarcastic.

Kindly, he slid his hand around my back to smooth over the
flesh of my round ass. "Well," he said, "I have a fantasy about
you fucking me. Your finger feels so good in my ass, but I want
to know what it's like to have more."

And, drumroll please, here is the more.

I clasp around the base of the shaft and press it to my crotch,
over my pants. *Do you ever wonder what it's like to have a dick?*
I repeat the question to myself, excited. Danny's the coolest
person I've ever dated. I lick my lips, which still taste like sugary
coffee and unemployment. I slam my laptop closed and peel off
my pants as I walk to my bedroom and kick the door shut.

The harness takes some puzzling—what goes where?—but the
sleek, dark leather feels good in my hands, soon kissing against
the outer lips of my cunt and sitting tight under my asscheeks.
I yank the steel hoop outward, which pulls on the straps, and I
roll my eyes back a little, loving it. I get hard from the struggle
to push the dildo inside the harness, watching it bend and flap
around obscenely.

Once it's in, I have a dick! I wag my hips back and forth,
looking over my tits and hips to watch the thing wag with me.
I go so fast that it slaps my thigh, and then I laugh. I stroke it,
pressing down so it rubs against my sex. I walk back and forth
through my apartment, catching myself in silver mirrors. I get
down on my hands and knees next to the tall mirror on the
bathroom door, and I watch myself touch this new thing that's
neither me nor not-me. I sit back with my legs bent and my
knees parted, and I pinch one nipple while stroking my labia
between strips of leather. I moan a little—leather! I trace my
fingers along the edge where it meets my flesh, purring. I tilt
my head back and grab some lube—why not? I drizzle a little

of the stuff onto the tip of my new dick and watch my fingers slide down. I add more, this time dripping it right on the cock and watching it move slowly down the shaft and pool at the bottom. Licking my lips, I guide the wet stuff over the steel ring and down to my cunt. I slide it over the petals of my sex, push my finger inside. I watch myself in the mirror, leaning forward to see my tits looking so good.

What will this feel like later tonight, when Danny's watching me do it? I imagine his fingers playing my labia while I do this to my cock. Will he ask me to fuck him? Will I know how to slide it in, how to go slow so that he can get used to me inside him like this? I imagine us switching back and forth—he's behind me, the new cock in one fist while the other rubs wetly up and down my pussy, sliding soft and tender against the supple-strong leather, while his hard sex is pressed to my asscheek. I'll grab around his waist and push him down on hands and knees, taking his cock in one hand while the other guides this thing to caress the sweet knot of muscle at the entrance to his ass, where I know a whole cavern of awesome pleasure begs for contact. I imagine him hesitating, nervous, even as he opens himself up for me, even as he asks me to enter him slowly, and as I imagine pushing into him, I rock the base against my clit and shove three fingers into my cunt. I work my thumb up under the harness to really get to my clit and I throw my head back and grind my hips until something big and shimmering lets loose inside me.

I hold myself still, savoring, breathing heavy. I pull my come-soaked fingers out of my cunt and use my own juice to slick up and down my new dick again. Later, I'll push Danny's mouth there, and make him lick it off.

I can hardly quit thinking about it. I put respectable clothes back on, and try writing cover letters at a coffee shop, but mostly I daydream. Danny wakes things up in me I didn't know were there. He's so observant, so curious. He taught me how to talk in bed—something I'd never been able to do before. "What does that feel like?" he'd ask me, fingering me, pressing and stroking different parts of my insides.

I'd pant and gasp and try answering, "Really good," or, "Yes, right there," but he wasn't satisfied.

"No," he'd say. "What does it *feel* like? Describe it to me!" he'd say, moving his finger to caress one particularly sensitive spot.

"Like swimming," I said once. "Like swimming in silver. When you press there, a silver wave hits."

He kissed my neck, held my ear between his teeth and told me deliciously dirty things. *When I touch you like this, your cunt gets so tight and wet. You're like a beautiful curtain, opening and closing on my hand, you're so luscious.*

At eight-thirty, half a cover letter later, I figure it's time to go. I pack my semi-functional laptop and notebook into a bag, and the barista, I think, catches the wistful half-smile subtle on my features. "Got any good plans for the night?" he asks.

His question makes me laugh. What if I told him, *I'm going to go pick up my boyfriend from the magic show where he works, and then I'm going to strip him naked and fuck him with the dick he brought home for me today?* But his eyes are sincere, probably lonely. "Thought I'd roast a chicken," I say, shrugging.

Once out the door, I crack up. Good euphemism.

Danny's more employed than me. He's been working for nearly fourteen years, right at the same place, with a few brief stints living in Portland and some off-seasons spent rambling. He's a stagehand in a magic show. That's right. He wears a majestic top hat, and he carries around silver trays laden with bunnies in various states of appearing and disappearing. He also does one third of the administrative work to run the strange old theater where the show plays. We met because he hired me—at the last "real" job I had—to do some restoration work and minor carpentry on the semi-historical interior. Now look at us.

He's dapper in his top hat, the black brim casting a dark shadow on his dark skin, the lush, dusky reds of the old theater framing him. When he sees me, he swoops the hat off and bows. I press up to him, and we waltz around the empty room, which still smells of popcorn and stale candy. He likes it when I lead, so I make him twirl and dip and then plant a soggy kiss on his cheek.

He leaves the top hat there—always much to my dismay, but on the walk home I get to see his dark eyes glitter against the still-wet streets, eyeliner smudged underneath, making him look smoky and mysterious.

"So," he says, taking me by the hand. "What did you think?"

I giggle, girlish.

"Did you try it out?" he asks. I appreciate him so much, walking beside me. He's so good at being himself. Tall, manly, with a feminine grace to his gestures, glisteningly healthy, dark skin and eyes and short little hairs he trims every few days. He looks so good, sometimes I get a little jealous of the audience watching him escort those magically appearing bunnies offstage on those silver trays. Of course, I can have complimentary entrance to the magic show any time I want, but that's beside the point.

"I did," I say, smiling wickedly.

"I've been thinking about it all day," he says, voice husky to prove it. An image flashes to mind of him accidentally taking the lid off a silver tray to reveal an upright cock, and I can hardly stop laughing long enough to describe it.

* * *

We stop for a bottle of white wine and take our time over dinner. Since I told him about the private joke I made at the barista, we decide we might as well follow through and roast some chicken. I get impatient, pacing around my apartment, picking up mugs of old tea and carrying them to the sink.

Danny's calm, making wild rice, whistling. He refills my wineglass and kisses the back of my neck. When I start to talk about my pathetic job search, he tilts his head empathetically and then says, "Do you want to talk about that? Or do you want me to distract you with something else?"

I punch him a little bit, and he pulls a tiny, silver animal—a unicorn, I see—from behind my ear. When I laugh, he closes his hand around it and then when he opens it again the unicorn is gone. I know I'll find it later, sometime when I'm not expecting— in the sugar bowl, or inside the toilet paper tube; it will fall out when I go to replace the roll. These tiny tricks surround me now, break down the seriousness of survival on the face of craggy life. Danny pulls little flashes of light from nowhere, and I'm transmuted from a lost ant into a bloom, a Ferris wheel, a thunderstorm, a cherry on top.

After dinner, pretty tipsy, we crowd into the tiny bathroom in my apartment and strip down. I turn on the shower and I'm already wet with soap in my hands when Danny climbs in after me.

Sometimes, when you've loved someone for a little while, you forget, and then you remember, and so it hits me, dizzyingly, that nowhere else in the world is there a person like that inside a body like this. Only here. When we met, I was at the office, just back from a worksite, and I had white paint speckles all over my cheeks, interspersed with freckles. I'd been single and repressed, no touch had ignited my curiosity in over a year, and Danny flashed this smile, and I knew I'd have him or nothing. *Maybe you could teach me some magic sometime*, I told him, touching a daub of wet paint onto his arm.

Amid steam and heat, I rub white soapsuds over him, watching his skin appear and disappear, running my lips over his chest when he's clean, appreciating the high contrast between his rich skin and my translucent freckles.

He stands behind me, curling his arms down my front, rubbing soap over my tits, letting the hot water wash it away. I part my legs and press my ass against him.

"May," he whispers. "You're gorgeous." He kisses my neck, strokes my cunt with two fingers, finding me so wet. "You're excited," he says, fondly.

I lean back against him awhile, relaxing into his caresses, until I push him away and get right down into the stream of water and reach for his cock. Danny's so hard and sweet, cardamom and mahogany, magic and dusk, and I take him into my mouth with the hot water and steam swirling around me. His hands twine in my wet hair, and I hear him gasp when I slide my tongue around on the underside of his shaft.

"Just a taste," I say, coming up.

While I towel off my hair, Danny heads to my room. He lights a bunch of candles, so that when I walk in, he's bathed in gold. I feel a little nervous, suddenly. Was I supposed to strap the dick on when he wasn't looking, and reappear as this alternate, dick-having self? Or does he want to watch me put it on? Does he want to help? He stretches out on my bed, watching me.

"You gonna come here? Or what?" he says.

I lie down next to him, and feel his big, slender hands strum over my body until I'm vibrating with heat. "Well," I say, "Do you want to try it out?"

He laughs. "I'm nervous," he says, reaching for the last few sips of a glass of wine he brought in here.

I run fingers up and down his chest, kissing the tops of his shoulders. I climb on top of him, straddling his middle, guiding his hands to touch my tits and hips. "Nervous, huh? We'll take it slow, baby. You can talk to me."

His teeth flash in a smile, which turns to a tiny growl. He pinches my nipple, holds my breast softly.

"Let's see here," I say, backing up. "Do you want to watch me put it on?"

He nods, smile half-devilish.

I pull the thing out of my underwear drawer, dick already inserted in ring. I make a performance of it, showing it to him. He leans on one elbow, legs stretched out, and starts to stroke his cock, curiosity sparkling in his dark eyes.

Things inside me start to tighten up and swell, my whole body an erection. I turn around, offering him a view of me situating the straps around my ass, giving them a good, firm tug. "Mmm," I groan a little, leather around my pussy. I lick my palm until it's slippery, and turn around to face him while I grip the new dick.

"Whoa," he says. His hand closes around his shaft, his tip twitching and swelling outward at me. I watch, mesmerized, trying to feel as if somehow his sensations are magically transmuted across space into the silicone flesh, so that I feel his pleasure through this extension strapped to my body.

Drunk with it, I whisper, "Stay put." I get off the bed and turn my back to him, one foot on the edge of the frame and the other bracing me from the floor, my ass facing Danny. He can curl his vision around, see the dick between my legs, see the leather straps frame my ass.

"Holy shit, May," he whispers. "That's so hot. Do you like how it feels?"

I pull on it, so that the leather gets tense around my sex. "This leather turns me on," I say. "Touch it."

He reaches fingers to slide over the edges of the straps, feeling where leather and skin meet. I widen my stance, inviting his fingers to find my cunt juicy and wet. He strokes, my labia contained between leather. It makes him moan. His hands sneak around, one at my pussy, the other at the dick. He pulls me back onto the bed and asks, "Is this how you want to be touched?"

"Like that," I say. His lips trail over my lower back as his fingers start to move inside of me and the cock wags up and down. "Pull on it, so the leather gets tight around my cunt," I command.

When he pulls, the straps yank around me and I groan.

"It's making you wet," he whispers.

"How hard are you?" I ask him. I turn to look. His cock stands at attention. I twist and manage to get a hand around him. I hold him tight while he massages my pussy, and I grow firmer, bolder, harder, needier, deep inside me, or outside me, as if I'm simultaneously expanding and contracting. Blue flowers blossom behind my eyes, and Danny's fingers slip away from my cunt.

"More!" I gasp.

He laughs. I take ahold of his cock. "You want my fingers? You want me to make you come already?"

"Yes!" His arms wrap around so that he's behind me, his hard thing resting along my asscrack, one hand gripping the dick and the other stroking my pussy. He presses two fingers inside, and rocks his hand against my need until everything starts to turn inside out, and I arch my back and tense my core and breathe so deep that I explode into a zillion tiny points of light.

But I waste no time on satisfaction. I twist around, putting my hands all over Danny's hot skin. "Baby," I tell him. "That was fantastic." I kiss his sweet lips, push my tongue between his teeth. I shove him down, get him onto his back, and kneel with one knee on either side of him. The dick wags and dangles between my legs, an obscene weight, right over his chest. I press three fingers into my pussy, still pulsing, and draw out fingerfuls of silky wet come. I watch him watch me slick the stuff over the dick, and with my other hand I caress his face. "Want a taste?" I ask, nasty.

He sticks out his tongue, and I guide the dick there, pressing my tits together with my other hand. He licks all over, grinning wickedly. "You!" he says, so pleased with me.

Then I shove Danny's legs apart and kneel between them. "Lube me up," I tell him, tilting my chin to the bottle of it, placed next to the bed.

"Yessir," grins Danny, turning the bottle upside down and drizzling a generous amount onto my hands. "Can I touch you here?" I ask him, gently sliding a finger up under his balls, between his asscheeks. "Is that what you want?"

"Mm-hmm," he says. His cock twitches, the tip pulsing, a bead of precome gathering like sensuous dew. I lick it, adding pressure with my tongue, and then slide my other palm up and down his shaft. Carefully, I find his asshole with the tip of my middle finger. I swirl lube around him, then I watch his features contort and relax as I slowly press my finger inside. "May!" he cries out, elated. Very gently, I move my finger in and out in tiny increments at his entrance, and at the same time I curl my finger and press up. Danny's hips rock a little, and then bear down. "Yes!" he whispers, needing.

"I'm getting you ready," I tell him, taking the dick in hand. "Do you want that? Do you want me to fuck you with this cock?" I punctuate my question with a deep caress of his prostate, making him moan and writhe. His sex is so hard—for half a second, I want it in me, instead of the other way around.

But when Danny widens his glittering eyes and I take in the whole sight of him in the candlelight, I'm so excited about giving him what he wants that I let go of my dick and take his into my mouth. Like this, I stroke deep inside him with one finger, and suck him while he watches my lips loving his shaft. "You want it?" I ask, holding his cock against my cheek.

"Please, baby," he says. "Give it to me."

"Good." I slip my finger out and he moans, twitching. "Turn around," I tell him. "Hands and knees."

He does it, happy. I kneel behind him, smooth my hand over his muscly ass. I give it a good smack, and then I grip his cock in one hand while I drip an impressive quantity of lube onto the dick. A generous sense of power surges through me, a kindness. "Danny baby," I tell him. "You're amazing." I caress his back, his legs. I find his entrance, and rest the tip of the dick there, giving him time.

"Touch me," he whispers. I find his cock, and touch him tenderly, gently rubbing myself over his crack, around the knot of muscle that waits for me to enter. "Okay," he sighs, "Go inside."

I tense up my cunt, feeling its sex and its power surge into the dildo, my life force pouring into Danny as I open him up and slide so carefully inside, a centimeter, an inch, a little more. Danny gasps and tenses up. "You okay?" I ask him, stroking his cock with a lubed hand, caressing the underside of his shaft.

"Uh-huh," he says, softly. I hold him for a long second, until he says, "Give me more."

I press in a little more, and then all at once Danny bucks his hips and presses back, burying this dick deep.

I make love, experimenting in gentle thrusts, tipping my pelvis up and down, imagining how the pressure must feel, finding the secret room inside of him, the place where desire performs, where shapes exchange their boundaries for pleasure. I think of the tiny interweavings of mysterious designs in gold leaf on his theater walls, the rich brocaded curtains, lush magic swirling, candlelight. Danny knows no mere sleight of hand, but a magic transformation where we are more than ourselves, dissolving and sighing, switching places and trying to extend past the edges of our skin. I hold myself still against him, gripping his sex, clasping him, and he rocks back and forth onto me, tingling and swelling and falling open slow and wild. A wind comes inside, billowing the curtains and setting the candles to shuddering. They let go of their light, and the room goes from gold to sliver, a high moon perfect on Danny's blue skin. I fall onto his back, clasp around his chest and let everything melt and slide together, stars gathering and spewing into constellations etched for such a pretty trick of love.

THE KISSING PARTY

Rachel Kramer Bussel

Who could resist an invitation to a kissing party? Not me. Some people think that kinky people only like the naughty parts of sex, the whips and chains and spankings, the crawling on the floor, the lips pried apart, the nipple clamps, the commands. I love all those things, but I love my husband Derek's beautiful lips more than anything. I could kiss them for hours—and I planned to, when he forwarded me the invitation to the kissing party. Over the years, we've been to our share of swingers clubs, sex parties, and play parties, not to mention the random dinner parties that, after dessert and a few glasses of wine, had turned into mini-orgies, but a kissing party would be something new. From what I could tell, the rules were that you could, and were encouraged to, kiss with abandon, but full-on sexual activity was verboten. How handsy we were allowed to get was up in the air, but I had a feeling we'd find out.

But we are, both of us, kinky to a fault, so he brought a blindfold and, yes, nipple clamps. He put the clamps on me at home, right before I got dressed, lovingly attaching each, then screwing them in. "I'm using these instead of the tweezer clamps so they don't get jostled; it wouldn't be the same if your pretty nipples were set free." So with my nipples trapped between the metal, and our other toys in my purse, we headed off in a cab for Brooklyn, a good half hour ride, with plenty of potholes, along with some jiggling from Derek. By the time we pulled up in front of the bar, I was so wet I almost wanted to go home, or sneak off to an alley where he could give me some relief.

"I thought you wanted to go to a kissing party, Belinda," he teased me, tipping the driver double our fare as he reached his hand down my black wrap dress and gave the man behind the wheel a peek at my nipple. I noticed him smile before Derek pulled me out of the cab.

"I do want to go, baby, but I don't know if I can wear these all night."

"Oh, you can, Belinda, and you will," he said, pulling me close for a kiss that started with my lips slammed hard against his, and ended with him biting my lower lip hard enough to make me whimper. I hurried up the stairs after him as best I could in my towering four-inch black-and-silver heels, my sexiest shoes, ones that conveniently pushed my ass out and my tits forward. Derek paid our entrance fee and ushered me into a lush bar with red-painted walls and erotic art on the walls.

Couples were kissing on bar stools, against doorways, in seats. And not just couples; I saw triple kisses and groupings, foursomes, and one lucky man lay across the laps of three beautiful women, one of whom was leaning down to kiss him. With a hand cupping my ass, Derek led me to the bar. Usually I'd order an extra-dirty martini, but when he ordered me a vodka and cranberry, then turned me around and began to blindfold me, I immediately knew why. I love the elegance of a martini glass, its sleek curves and olive decoration, but trying to drink out of one without seeing what I was holding would surely lead to a martini-soaked dress. Plus Derek likes seeing me put anything in my mouth, mini-straws included.

"And for the lady," the bartender said, making my face warm when I turned back in my seat, knowing the word emblazoned on the blindfold would tell him everything he needed to know about me: slut. It was true—for Derek, I was a slut in the very best sense of the word. I'd do anything he asked me to, even if I didn't initially like it, even if it embarrassed me or made me nervous. I love and trust him, and he's never steered me wrong.

"Thank you," I said when Derek pinched my ass, then put my hand out for my drink, but Derek slapped it away.

"Not tonight, my slut." I heard him rummaging around in my bag and seconds later found my wrists being fastened into leather handcuffs behind my back. He must have slipped them in my bag when I wasn't looking. He returned to his stool and said, "Now you can open that pretty mouth," and when I did, he slipped the straw in. It may not seem like such a big deal, sipping a drink from a straw, especially in a room full of people kissing, but when you're wearing a slut blindfold, nipple clamps and handcuffs in public, it becomes a pretty big deal—big enough to make my pussy ache. I took a big sip and then let the straw go.

No sooner were my lips free than Derek was tilting my head toward his and kissing me again. This kiss wasn't like the one we'd shared outdoors. It was soft and slow and tender, his tongue making love to mine, filling me with warmth. I angled closer, tilting my head, taking him in. His hands moved to my cheeks and his tongue took over, invading so I almost couldn't breathe. The kiss finally ended, leaving me trembling. "You have fans, Belinda," he whispered in my ear. "I can see several couples checking you out, admiring how hot you look. I think the friendly thing to do would be to offer to kiss them, don't you?" Of course it wasn't really a question—it never is with Derek. He was telling me that I was about to kiss strangers I couldn't see, under his tutelage.

He gave my cheek a little pat, then a slightly harder one. I moaned, knowing this wasn't the time or place for a full-on slapping session, the kind that leads to him tossing me onto the bed, shoving my ankles up to his hips, and fucking me as hard as he can. Maybe I'd be lucky and get that later. Now it was kissing time.

Derek moved behind me and helped me stand up, keeping an arm around my waist to balance me as I walked in the heels. I heard him say hello to a table of people, then thrust me forward. "This is Belinda. She's mine, but I'm offering her to you to kiss and pet. She likes being used like that, and she's very good with her mouth. Feel free to kiss her here, too," he finished, exposing my clamped nipples, which by then were throbbing.

"Hi, Belinda," cooed a woman's voice. I pictured her with teased bleached-blonde hair and glossy red lips, a modern-day Marilyn Monroe. Her sweet perfume suffused my senses, and soon I was sitting down next to her while her lips met mine. Her lips were sticky with gloss, her tongue tentative at first. I heard murmurings around me but was too focused on the kiss to make out the conversations. The woman's hands brushed the skirt of my dress open enough to expose the fact that I wasn't wearing panties. She left it like that, and kept kissing me, her tongue tickling mine, her gloss smearing into my skin.

Since her hands were tangled in my long brown hair, I knew someone else must have reached for my nipples, thumbs massaging them, rotating each clamped nub. As the touch permeated my body, sending waves of pleasure starting from my nipples and radiating outward, I realized it didn't matter who was touching me. Maybe it was even hotter not to know, not to think, to simply feel. "You can take them off if you want to," I heard Derek say. No one else had ever shared that honor since we'd started dating, and he hadn't told me he planned to allow that. Maybe it was spontaneous. I wasn't sure how I felt about that, but the woman's lips and the mystery hands felt so good, I didn't even think about protesting. Besides, I knew what protesting Derek's plans usually got me, and I wanted to savor the moment.

I tried to prepare myself for the rush of blood about to flood my tender flattened buds, but you can never truly be ready. That's part of the thrill of kink for me—the unexpected, the way even the most familiar activity can catch you off guard, make you feel like a virgin all over again as the pain crashes down.

I felt heady as the woman kissed me deeply, her hands on my cheeks, her perfume invading my senses as my nipples got reacquainted with their freedom. They only had a few moments before someone took one breast in his or her hand and started sucking my nipple. Derek whispered my name in my right ear, a reminder, a warning, a promise. He can make my name sound like the most beautiful aria or the most dreaded epithet, and he knows me well enough to know that in the right circumstances, both of those turn me on.

Then he was kissing the back of my neck, his lips warm, his stubble brushing my skin. I almost laughed at the sensual overload, my dress still splayed open, leaving my pussy on display, while three sets of lips devoured me. Derek's tongue brushed lightly against my neck, a tender contrast to the woman's tongue pressing deep into my mouth and the mouth now sucking deeply on my nipple before biting it just enough to make me gasp.

"Is she being a good slut for you?" Derek asked, loud enough to surely draw the attention of anyone who hadn't already been watching us. "You should see what she looks like with a cock in her mouth and one in her pussy. My girl is happy as long as she has something to fill those pretty lips." No sooner had Derek made that pronouncement than my pussy clenched, making me wonder if I was dripping onto the seat beneath me. The other mouths on me quickly separated from me, leaving my nipple wet and needy, my mouth empty. I rearranged myself as best I could, trapped by the cuffs. I could talk, but what would I ask for? Derek surely knew what I wanted, and I was getting increasingly antsy for him to take me outside and give it to me.

Instead I felt his fingers, four of them, fucking my mouth, making me focus all my energy on stretching around him. He was showing me off, teasing the crowd, making sure they knew exactly how far my oral charms extended. We weren't kissing, but I had a feeling that didn't quite matter by then. We'd already broken a few rules, so perhaps they were ones the crowd had been waiting for to be broken. He kept his fingers in my mouth, but stilled them, so I was left to simply suck and salivate while I listened to the unmistakable sound of him kissing the woman, hearing the same murmurs she'd just made while kissing me. I wondered if he wanted to do more than kiss her, though I would've bet money she wanted to do more than kiss him. I could tell from the noises she was making, the whimpers coming from somewhere deep inside.

"Kiss her again," Derek said, and soon her lips were pressing hard against me. I pictured his hand on her neck, pushing her against me, mashing our mouths together. "It's too bad Belinda has to leave soon so I can make sure she gets fucked good and hard. Maybe I'll have to strap a vibrator inside her next time we attend this party so she can be a little more patient. Give her a hickey as a souvenir," he ordered gruffly, and in seconds the woman's mouth was fastened to my neck, biting hard. I shuddered, surprised he'd let anyone else do that to me.

"Thank you all," Derek said, before he ushered me to my feet and led me away from the table. I'd thought maybe he'd let me see who I'd been kissing, who'd been touching and sucking my nipples, who'd been watching me. Instead he led me to the doorway and only once I felt the promise of the cool air did he undo the cuffs and take off the blindfold. "Kiss me," he commanded, his lips warm, sweet and brutal—just the way I like them.

One newly freed hand found its way to his cock, hard and warm beneath his pants. "I'm not done with you," he told me, as he led me out the door. Now I could see, and hold his hand, but a part of me was still floating, caught up in the high of being on display, being kissed and sucked and used, but only being able to return a fraction of those touches. We quickly reached an alley he seemed to know well, leading me far enough from the street that we couldn't be seen unless someone walked directly past.

"Stand right there," Derek ordered, and lest I expect to keep my mobility, he raised my arms above my head and refastened the cuffs. "Put your arms around my neck." We just fit, him pressed tight against me as he lifted my dress and shoved his fingers inside me. I buried my face in his neck as he fucked me, more ready than I'd realized. In no time I was trembling against him, grateful for the extra support of the wall behind me and his body pressed right up against mine. He kissed me roughly, stealing my breath for a few moments as I came against his fingers, which he quickly withdrew. He undid my arms from his neck and clamped his hand over my mouth as I kept on trembling. I was still so wet and open, and when he let me taste myself on his fingers, I hoped he'd give me his cock next.

But when I'm tied up, when I'm cuffed, when I can't move,

Derek likes to make sure I'm fully aware of exactly whose control I'm under. I knew he'd probably love to fuck me right there, pound me into the wall, let my bare ass brush against its coldness, but instead he rearranged me so my bare breasts were hanging out, my dress barely more than a wispy decoration.

With my arms clamped in front of me and my tits hanging between them, he pushed me to my knees, my legs tucked under me, wet slit pressed against my calves. I watched him take out his cock. I immediately stuck out my tongue, hungry to taste him, but even that he wanted to deny me. "I know you wish everyone from the party were here to watch you suck my cock, but they're not. Nobody's here to see what I'm about to do to you." He stroked his cock slowly, teasing me by bringing it so close to my outstretched tongue, letting its dripping head brush once against me before stepping just out of reach. I put my tongue back in my mouth. He hovered over me, aiming his dick right at my tits. It didn't take long before he was groaning, covering my breasts, my cuffs, my fingers and my dress with his come.

He scooped some up and fed it to me, then pulled me up by my joined wrists before unbuckling them. I knew full well he knew I always carry wipes in my purse, but he didn't offer to let me get one out. Instead he took my face gently in one hand and kissed me, while twisting one nipple with the other. He kept kissing me even as he undid the cuffs, tossing them on the ground before returning to greet my lips with his. His sweet, soft kiss combined with his harsh grip, even with his cream coating me, had me aching to touch myself again. With Derek, though, I don't need to be tied up to know when I'm allowed to move. If he wanted me to touch myself, he'd tell me to. Instead I kissed him back until he was done, then covered myself as best I could. He let me put on a sweater and led me to a taxi.

Inside, he smiled at me, recounting our entire evening in a

voice loud enough for the driver to overhear. "Maybe we should host our own kissing party," he said as we neared our door.

"Any time," I told him, as I headed up the stairs, his hand on my ass, promising me our night wasn't over yet.

A NOT-SO-SUBTLE SPICE

Alison Tyler

Bent over, bottom exposed in the split of the leggings, plump arsecheeks.

There was a time when I read Victorian pornography that I kept hidden beneath my mattress so my husband wouldn't know. I'd bought the book at a secondhand store—clearly shelved by accident with the mysteries. The title had piqued my interest, and when I pulled the tome from the shelf, the fat spine split open, and I found myself mesmerized by the text on the yellowing pages.

Words leaped out at me: *birching, pantaloons, figging, flogging, martinet.* I knew what some meant, didn't understand others. I'd only read a few paragraphs, growing wetter and wetter with each sentence, before deciding I needed to own the book.

I paid for my purchase and immediately left the store on shaky legs. I couldn't even wait to get home. I hurried to my car parked in the dusty little parking lot behind the bookstore, and I fell inside the driver's seat, trembling all over. I'd never read anything like this before. With no control of myself, I slid my fingers under my dress and into my panties. I devoured the stories about taboo topics—the printing odd and almost indecipherable in places, the descriptions of the undergarments like something from a twisted lingerie catalog.

My car was parked beneath a magnolia tree. Late afternoon sunlight spilled through the purple-tinged white petals, heating their scent. I couldn't catch my breath. I couldn't stop myself. I leaned into the steering wheel, groaning as the climax took me.

That was my first.

I'd seen porn before, of course. Everyone had spied the stack of *Playboys* kept in the garage or in a toolshed—even mild-mannered housewives such as myself. But the models in those spreads were blonde and shiny and clean. Their bios were penned in darling handwriting as they confessed a love of strawberry ice cream and sunset walks on a white-sand beach. These stories were filled with secret longings, dark desires.

Birch rods, quim, flog, spirit, naughty, cocks.

I was supposed to buy Hamburger Helper at the grocery store, to have my husband's ice-cold Bud on the Formica table when he came home from work. But I couldn't make myself.

Wide-open cunt, lovely bottom hole.

I skipped the store.

At home, I touched myself to story after story. I had never done this before. I knew men masturbated—it was something they did for release—but I hadn't felt the urge. Now I was in a frenzy. The pieces had been originally printed as serials—and the layout of the collection was true to the publication. So in order to read an entire story from start to finish, one had to flip forward, trying to find the next installment, trying to devour the whole situation. A naughty maid, soundly punished for a minor indiscretion—figged—there was that word again—to keep her from clenching.

Clenching *how*? Clenching *what*?

The time got away from me. I made Sloppy Joes at the last possible minute, an old standby and Henry didn't seem to notice. He didn't smell my scent on my fingers. I'd scrubbed myself fiercely after climaxing for the fourth time—and my skin was tinted pale green under my nails from Palmolive. Henry bent and lightly pressed his lips to my cheek before taking a second beer to the living room to watch TV. And that was that for us. That was that for the night, except for the occasional call for a fresh Bud.

I washed the dishes. Then I sat at the table and waited for him to go to sleep, needing to read more of the book. Taking the book into the closet with me, sitting by Henry's work boots and trying to figure out every phrase in the story. Henry rolled over heavily in the bed, and I started, then snuck the book to the living room, reading curled up on one corner of the settee until I'd finished the whole thing, breathless and confused.

This was a fairy-tale collection. That's how the stories read to me. Taboo fantasies that could never come true.

Until...

I went to the library to research figging. I was desperate, my panties wet as I learned more about the term. I unraveled the mystery slowly. The way the piece of ginger was peeled and often kept in a glass of water until the appropriate moment of use. Appropriate. What a word to go with the act of sliding a fresh piece of ginger into a woman's asshole. The way a naughty miscreant would be bent over and forced to hold her asscheeks apart for the insertion.

Oh, sweet mother of mercy, insertion.

Finding a grocery that sold ginger root and not powdered ginger in sanitary bottles was difficult. I had to drive thirty minutes to a specialty store and purchase the knobby, gnarled bulb. By then, I was keeping my battered copy of the Victorian erotica in my handbag, stealing moments in alleys, on shady streets, reading and rereading the words until I had entire passages memorized.

I stashed the root in the vegetable crisper, certain that Henry would never discover my secret. He was a simple man with simple tastes, both easy to anticipate and to please. He was fine with my chipped beef on toast, happy with a tuna casserole, grateful every time I mixed Lipton soup mix into sour cream to create his favorite dip. If he sensed a change in my behavior, he didn't let on. We made a good team—we always had, and if—as people say—variety is the spice of life, then we were both satisfied with life on the bland side. A little salt. Not too much pepper. Nothing unexpected, foreign or gourmet.

We had a routine. He went to work, and he put in a full eight hours. I kept the house, and that meant something. There was dusting, vacuuming, gardening, making his meals, ironing his shirts. My days were filled—at least, they always had been—until I found the book.

I sat in the kitchen late at night, fondling the root while he slept, wondering if I'd have the nerve, if I might take the parer to the tanned digit-like protuberance and shave away the thick skin. I imagined what the ginger would taste like if I sucked the tip into my mouth. I fantasized how the root would feel if I got up the nerve to put the thing where I wanted it most.

But soon I needed more. The stories all described the clothing—pantaloons or pantalettes with ruffles at the edges, undergarments that split and tied. I went to secondhand stores, then costume shops, then finally to vintage stores I found listed at the back of the *Yellow Pages*. I searched until I located the closest pieces I could to the ones featured in the tales. I coupon-shopped and scrimped and saved until I could afford one pair of underwear—old-fashioned with ribbons that laced and a seam at the crotch that would part like a ripe peach and reveal the nakedness beneath.

And oh, dear lord I will confess to clutching that garment in my hands, awash in shivers as I brought the crisp material to my face, breathing in the scent of laundry soap and rose sachets.

By then my ginger had shriveled and wilted, from age I knew, but I felt somehow it was from lack of use. I had to return to the store once more—that thirty-minute drive like one long bout of foreplay—to buy a fresh root, an even larger one this time.

The next day, I waited until Henry left for work and put on a white sundress. I took off my nylon hip-hugger underpants and slid into the pantaloons. I did my hair in braids with ribbons at the end and added only spots of petal blush on my cheekbones and bit my lips hard to bring up a natural red.

Turning in front of the mirror I told myself the story. Henry, searching for beer one night, would find the root and ask, "What's this, doll baby?" The root would almost disappear in his big fist, the question would illuminate his sky-blue eyes. He understood carrots and potatoes, frozen peas and creamed corn. An odd-shaped root like this would have no meaning to him.

"What is this, Bonnie?" he'd ask me, and I recalled in a flash the time I'd bought a fancy type of lettuce instead of iceberg, and how he'd tried to eat it, pouring on the Thousand Island, wincing at the bitter taste. I'd purchased a head of iceberg the very next day.

What would he say if I shoved the book into his hands, if I begged him to do to me what the man did in the story to the bad wife with her rosy orifices and her need for birching before fucking.

I no longer considered that part of myself as my "pussy." In the stories, the sensual space between a woman's legs was always a cunt or a quim. I liked to say that word aloud: "quim," and mine was too wet at the thought. I sought release, relief, rushing to the kitchen and gripping up the ginger, paring the rough skin with a few forceful strokes. It was time. It was finally time. I submerged the naked root in ice water while I tried to catch my breath. I would do it myself. I would put the ginger up my ass and feel the slow burn. I'd read every bit of information I could gather about the act. How at first, there wouldn't be much pain at all. Then, slowly, I would understand the sensation intimately, the gradual heat that would build. And if I clenched, I would...

The kitchen door opened unexpectedly, and I gasped and dropped the blade into the stainless-steel sink. Henry, home only forty minutes after he'd departed, found me staring at him wild eyed, wearing an antique-looking costume, holding a spice from a far-off land.

"What's all this, doll baby?" he asked in his deep baritone, that soothing voice I'd loved the first time he spoke. Why was he home? I glanced over and saw his lunch box forgotten on the counter, the shiny metal reflecting my frightened expression. Henry came closer and I could see him taking in my odd outfit—the floaty dress, the ruffle of those pantaloons peeking out beneath, my hair done simply in an antique style. "What's this?" The root—odd-shaped but smooth now, almost glistening in the glass of water. And me...stammering and useless, robbed of all sense of speech.

I couldn't explain. All I could do was to show him—as I had in my fantasy—leading him to the bedroom, pulling out the battered old book, which fell open to my favorite page.

Henry looked shocked at first by the existence of the book. Why was I keeping a book under our mattress? And why was I such a wreck? Henry read the sports pages, and I knew he had a dirty magazine or two out in the garage, but I never saw him reach for a book that wasn't some sort of manual—fix the car, fix the water heater, fix the plumbing. Now he sat on the edge of our bed and he read the words, his lips moving along with them, his brow furrowed. I clasped and unclasped my hands. I moved back and forth from one foot to the other. Henry and I didn't talk about sex. Yes, we had intercourse, and that was the word I'd use—every Friday night. Sometimes Sunday mornings. We loved each other, but we didn't do this. Whatever *this* was. With me almost panting, my throat dry, my cheeks hot, with Henry squinting at the words as if willing them to make sense.

Then he tilted his head at me, and he smiled, and my stomach unknotted. He wasn't angry. He wasn't upset. He looked at me, and then he spun me around, so he could see the outfit. Face-to-face once more, he lifted up my dress, taking in the ruffles on the pantaloons, admiring the way the antique garment fit. Not sleek like the nylon briefs I wore daily, but slightly loose and beriboned at the rear.

"You want this," he said, and he motioned to the book discarded on the bed. He drew me closer, between his big thighs, and he stroked his hands over my braids and he kissed my bitten lips. "You want this." Not a question, not a flicker of judgment.

"Yes."

"Bend over the bed," he said, and that voice was gruff and raw, different sounding than I'd ever heard it speak. I gripped the blanket, a wedding gift. I stared at the tiny sprays of delicate daisies dancing over the pale-blue background. Henry left the room, and I knew where he was going, and I knew what this meant. He returned with the ginger, and he said, "It's going to burn."

"I know."

"You want it to burn."

"Yes."

He undid the ribbon at the back of the new/old knickers, and he parted the split and he held me open. I closed my eyes, then I felt him press the knobby head of that ginger root against my anal opening. We had had intercourse—that was the word. We had slept in the same bed, and he had put his penis in my vagina. But he had never put his fingers here, opening me, displaying me. And now, he was inserting the root, and I could feel the whisper of heat, growing bigger, growing bolder. I could feel the promise of the pain, and my cunt spasmed.

"You aren't meant to clench," he said, and he sounded intrigued and he sounded aroused. I looked over my shoulder at him as he reached for the book—*my* book—and read more. "But this is only the prelude, because now you need to be whipped."

We had eaten at the dining room table together. Sometimes talking about the weather or about what one of the men had told him at work—a used pickup truck for sale, a neighbor's son joining the military. We had talked, like husband and wife, like a couple. Like you do. And now he was unbuckling his belt and he was going to tan my backside while I didn't clench my cheeks around the ginger root slid up in there. My quim was dripping. I'd never thought much about how my cunt would feel when I imagined the ginger. I only concentrated on my ass. But the truth was that I could have come if I slid a finger between my nether lips, if I pressed down hard against my clit.

Henry, as if sensing my thoughts, leaned over me on the bed, his body pushing against mine so that the ginger slid even deeper into my ass. "Don't touch yourself," he said. "Don't even think about it."

I kept my hands on the blanket where he could see them. He rocked the ginger in and out of my behind, and my cheeks flamed pink.

"The point is to not clench," he said, "while I thrash you."

My heart pounded. I heard him snap his belt. I'd watched him thread that belt through the loops of his slacks for seven years. I had never thought he would ever use that strip of leather on my ass. He made the first blow count. I clenched unwittingly, and then I cried out. The burn intensified immediately, as the stories had said it would. "Ah, Bonnie," Henry said, and I could hear a smile in his tone. "That's exactly what you're *not* supposed to do. How'd that feel?"

I didn't answer. His big fist found my braids and pulled. I wasn't expecting that, him forcing me to turn my face to him. My eyes were tearing as I stared at him. "How'd that feel?" he repeated, and I whispered, "It hurt."

"Tell me."

"It's like fire inside me," I said in a rush.

He reached beneath my body and his fingertips strummed my clitoris. We had never—he had never—thought to ask about my pleasure. We had done it— the "it" being sex—the way we thought you should, the way we thought you were supposed to. But now Henry had his fingers on my button, and he was rubbing hard while the burning built inside me.

"I'm going to whip you again," he said, "and you're not going to clench this time."

"No, Henry," I whispered.

"No?"

"I mean, yes, Henry." I was out of my head with desire.

He struck me again, then again. I could hardly feel the pain from the belt on my skin because of the burning ginger in my ass. But I knew one thing. I knew that I needed this. My body was electrified like never before. I was panting, thrashing, squirming with every blow of his belt on my backside. Then he dropped the belt and he rocked the ginger into my ass by spanking with his palm repeatedly against the base of the root.

"Oh, oh!" I whimpered, and I thought of all the characters who cried out from pain and pleasure in my book. I had never made much noise in bed. Henry had never given me any reason to—and I hadn't thought to tell him how.

Just as the fire from the ginger started to dissipate, Henry pulled the root from my ass. He took off his clothes and got onto the mattress with me. I felt him probing me from behind, his cock sliding into the copious wetness between my legs. Then he thrust into me while running his fingers up and down my clit, and I came like a wild thing. The spasms of my cunt made Henry groan. He'd never been in me while I climaxed because I'd never climaxed during sex, and this was something new and exciting for him, too.

When he was slicked up with my juices, he pulled out and pressed this head of his cock to my asshole. "Do you want this, Bonnie?" he asked.

Oh, I did. So much. I thought of the words in my book, the characters crying out that they were dying when they were coming. I felt as desperate as they had sounded. Henry waited for me to say, "Yes, please, yes," and then he drove his cock into my sore and throbbing asshole and fucked me there as the last rays of the pain flickered away and a true, beautiful pleasure took over.

He kept using his fingers on my clit as he drove into my ass, and he waited to orgasm until he had taken me to another level. Only when I was delirious with pleasure, only when I was practically sobbing his name over and over did he let loose, filling me up with his seed.

When he pulled out, he got us both under the covers and he held me to him. "You're going to be late for work," I said, glancing at the clock on the bedside table. I wondered how we'd ever go back to normal now.

"Yes," Henry agreed. "I'm going to be late. In fact, I'm going to be late again and again today. I'm going to be so late as I fuck your ass, and whip your holes, and lick every inch of you."

I could feel the thrill building inside me once more. I hadn't known Henry could be like this. I recalled the time I had brought in the rogue lettuce, and I said softly, "I thought you liked a routine. I thought you liked simple."

He laughed and he tugged one of my braids, and he kissed my lips. He said, "Some changes *simply* take getting used to."

And then he was on me once more, kissing my lips, moving down my body to press his mouth between my legs—something he'd never done before, something I never wanted him to stop.

He was true to his word. He carried me to the shower and washed us both. He read aloud to me from my book, and he forced me to show him my treasured scenarios, so that he could bring the different ones to life. We spent all day fucking, until we were limp and useless and we had to go out to dinner for sustenance, sitting across from each other in the diner booth and laughing at our newfound secret. Henry added more pepper to his meal than I'd seen him do before.

When he arrived home from work the next night, Henry had a bag from the grocery store. I peeked in and saw a new type of cheese, not our standard Wisconsin cheddar, a bottle of wine, not a six-pack of beer, a box of gourmet cookies—not vanilla wafers. And a ginger root.

"You know," he said, as he lined up the groceries on the blue-and-white countertop. "I always *did* wonder what life would be like with a different kind of spice."

TRYST OF FATE

Lydia Hill

I'd been on the road for three tedious days, driving between Bumfuck, Oklahoma and Hicksville, Texas, on a sales trip that made me vacillate between quitting my job as Southwestern sales rep for Sweet Dreams Lingerie, or killing my boss. The temperature had hovered above one hundred for the three days I'd been stuck in the rental car. Then the power grid had been knocked out after a series of freak tornados, so when my car started knocking I lost reception right in the middle of my distress call to the rental company.

Now I was broken down in some desolate stretch of nowhere, and the only thing between me and sleeping in my car was a motel so ratty it rated zero stars. But I was out of options so I coasted into the dusty, unpaved parking lot and turned off the ignition, relieved at least to have made it that far.

The place looked deserted, but there was a dented old red Ford flatbed parked in front of the motel office, so I figured someone must be on the job. I pulled open the door and stepped inside.

I felt a wicked sizzle in my blood when the guy in the office looked up at me. He was the kind of man my mother warned me about. Not necessarily mad, but definitely bad and dangerous to know. There were circles of sweat in the armpits of the black T-shirt that was stretched tight across his muscled chest. He wore a pair of threadbare jeans and his bare feet were up on the desk. He needed a shave—had needed one several days ago, in fact. And he hadn't seen the inside of a barbershop in some time. Long, thick, tangled black hair framed hungry eyes and a sneer. If Heathcliff had been a Texas redneck he'd have looked like this guy.

"Listen, I'm broke down outside. I've tried calling the rental company but there's no reception so I need a room for the night."

He didn't respond. Just chuckled in an evil fashion as he took a swig from the open bottle of tequila dangling from his hand. He swallowed slowly, looking me up and down the entire time. I squirmed under the blatant once-over that made me feel like he was a starving hound and I was fresh meat.

"Room? Sure, you can have a room." He contemplated the ceiling and smiled. "Fifty bucks a night. Cash."

In my desperation it seemed like a steal. "Fine. Fifty. Here." I pulled out my wallet and handed over the bills. He tucked them into his pocket and reached toward a row of keys hanging on the wall.

"How 'bout a room by the pool?"

"Pool? You have a pool here?"

"'Course there ain't no water in it."

"Oh. Well, fine, whatever." His intense focus made me nervous and jittery so I snatched the key he offered and hurried out.

He hadn't lied. The room was next to the pool. The empty

pool filled with tumbleweeds and what looked like a dead animal carcass. I took a good look around the musty room, disgusted with the grime and what looked suspiciously like mouse turds in the corners. I couldn't seem to catch a break. Sitting alone on the bed in the nasty room I decided being an independent and take-charge woman sucked.

I mustered the energy to go into the dingy bathroom to wash, hoping it might cool me down a little, only to discover there was no running water either. I cursed and stomped around for a while, then stripped and changed into my lightest summer dress, telling myself it was only for the sake of comfort in the heat that I didn't put on undies. I slid on my flip-flops and went hunting for the manager.

The office was wide open and deserted. The Ford was still parked crookedly in front, so I wandered around back until I came to a stand of pines that shaded the back rooms. Heathcliff was lounging on a cot, watching the sunset and enjoying his tequila.

"Excuse me?"

He turned and looked hard at me. He was leaning against the wall of the motel with one hand in his lap and as he stared, he casually began to stroke himself. His impressive hard-on was riveting, and I couldn't ignore it.

"There's no running water."

"No shit. Power's been off since yesterday afternoon and the water's pumped from a well. No electric, no pump, no water. Life sucks and then you die." He took another healthy swallow of liquor.

At that moment the sun disappeared behind the distant mountains and the dimness of twilight settled over us. A sense of expectation hung in the sultry air. He continued to fondle himself and since the whole thing was miles outside my comfort zone, I retreated back to my room. I locked the door, lay down on the bed and prayed for morning.

Night fell and though the heat of day had dissipated, the room was still stifling. The air was gritty and stale, and opening the tiny, grimy window didn't help. I twisted on the bed, uncomfortable and tense. Worse, the image of Heathcliff masturbating as he lay on the cot was burned into my brain. I kept imagining what his cock looked like. Remembering the look in his eyes as he stared at me, I felt like a caged animal desperate to escape captivity. My heart thumped loudly in the twilight until I gave up the fight. I surrendered to the mounting urges, and went back outside, breathing a little bit faster.

"Hot night."

Heathcliff was sitting exactly as I'd left him an hour earlier. He looked at me with a feral smile and held out the half-empty bottle of tequila. "Drink?"

A powerful awareness crackled between us, and I felt the trickle of moisture seeping between my thighs. He was low class and crude, and all I could think of was how desperately I wanted him to fuck me.

He'd lit a couple of torches and the flames flickered in the breeze, throwing eerie shadows around us. It created a starkly pagan atmosphere, as if my mundane, civilized world had ceased to exist when I stepped out of my car. My pussy clenched as I stood there in the steamy night.

I reached out and wrapped my hand around the bottle of tequila. As intently as a predator, he watched as I raised it to my mouth and took a deep swallow. I could taste him on the bottle, the sharp tang of sweat and tobacco from his lips more intoxicating than the booze. I took a second slug and handed him back the bottle.

He stroked his cock lazily through his jeans and his gaze never wavered. I felt dizzy and breathless.

"Sit." He slid over on the cot, leaving just enough space for me to squeeze next to him. I was acting crazy, but common sense had abandoned me. I was overwhelmed by the unquenchable desire to have him on top of me, have him inside of me. To feel him ramming his cock into me without mercy until I screamed.

I lowered myself next to him on the worn mattress, itchy with need. I let out a breath I didn't know I was holding when he slid the large hand off his erection and onto my thigh.

"Pretty." Fingers plucked at the soft, pale-pink fabric of my summery dress. It looked innocent and virginal beneath his dark, rough hand. I stared at a brutal puckered scar that stretched all the way up his forearm and wondered what violence he'd suffered. He slowly slid the fabric up my thighs, calloused fingertips skimming over my bare knees. As he stroked my skin, his touch grew rough and possessive and his fingers inched toward the juncture of my thighs where moisture pooled. I shivered in expectation.

This would be no genteel interlude. He was no staid businessman seducing me after dinner and cocktails. There'd be no bed covered in pristine sheets in a climate-controlled environment. I would not be having a sedate orgasm before getting a sterile good-night kiss. The anticipation of the unknown made it all the more arousing. I'd abandoned my poised indifference along with my silk and pearls. I was lying there wet and quivering with lust, waiting impatiently to be screwed senseless by this dark, linguistically challenged stranger.

His fingers moved by infinitesimal degrees. Insidious sensations crept through me until every cell of my being was bursting with want. I watched his hand as it moved, as he pushed my dress up to my hips, across my lap, exposing me.

"That is one sweet little snatch." He slid one fingertip between my dripping labia and rubbed it back and forth through the slickness, before putting his finger to his lips and sucking. His eyes closed and he groaned.

"Man, I missed that." He slid off the cot onto his knees, grabbed my thighs and thrust them apart. His eyes glittered hungrily as he stared at my pussy, spread wide open for him.

"Now you just lie still while I eat you up." He bent between my legs and his hot lips latched on to my clit and started sucking. I let go of the last whisper of sanity and gave myself over to the explosive feelings. His tongue was forceful, his lips and teeth brutal as he bit and sucked and licked. He pushed his tongue deep into my cunt, lapping at me like a hungry dog. Slurping sounds broke the silence as he fucked me with his mouth and I whimpered ecstatically every time he bit down on my turgid clit.

His hands tightened on my thighs and he held me down as he suckled my flesh. It was a pleasure so immense it was painful. I clenched my hands on the metal frame of the cot, my entire world centered between my thighs as my orgasm began to build. It grew until it crested like a sleek wave, and I gasped when it streamed over me with a heated sizzle in the summer night.

He sat back on his haunches and licked his lips like a glutton finishing a delicious meal. I stared at him beneath half-closed eyes as he crawled back on the cot until he was looming over me. He pulled off his T-shirt, revealing a tattooed chest so tight and muscular I could have bounced a quarter off it.

"Off." He yanked at my dress and tossed it impatiently aside, then roughly grabbed hold of my tits with greedy hands, twisting and pulling harshly. Grinning darkly, he pinched my nipples until they were standing up, stiff little peaks of desire. He lazily slapped one breast, then the other, leaving sharp red marks, and I felt a brutal responding tug of hunger in my cunt.

He mesmerized me. What should have disgusted me aroused me. What should have been frightening was alluring. In the distance a brilliant arc of lightning coursed through the night sky as if to punctuate the need pulsing through my body.

He slid his jeans off and freed his cock. It was long, thick and angry. He jerked at it with one hand while he continued to torment my tits with the other. He bent over and sucked a nipple into his mouth and drew hard on it. The bristle of his days' old beard rasped over my flesh like sandpaper, sensitizing it, heightening all the sensations that his lips and teeth and tongue and hands were eliciting. He was voracious. He left hickeys and teeth marks all over one breast, then the other, biting at my nipples until it was glorious and nearly unbearable.

I writhed and begged. "Please please please fuck me fuck me." The lusty litany spilling from my lips stopped only when he rammed his cock balls deep inside me.

"God, oh god." I clutched my ankles around his ass as he fucked me, grunting and pounding into me like a raging animal. He impaled me again and again as I lay beneath him, reveling in the erotic, liquid slap of our bodies. When he reared up and shot his come deep inside of me I shuddered uncontrollably and this time I came screaming.

Just as suddenly as he'd rammed into me, he pulled out. He stood up in front of me, grabbed me by the hair and pulled me up until I was sitting on the edge of the cot. His organ quivered in front of me, wet with our juices, and he grabbed my jaw and squeezed.

"I've waited a long time for this." His voice was husky and rough, like the sex. He didn't wait for permission. He shoved his cock into my mouth and growled, "Suck me." I tasted myself on him as he rammed his length down my throat. My jaw ached with the strain of being forced open wide as he fucked my face and I gagged around him but he never slowed. He continued to slam his cock into my mouth until his balls slapped against my chin. Drool ran out of my mouth as he held my head immobile, while I desperately sucked and swallowed, trying to take him deeper.

It was the most nasty, decadent, mind-blowing experience of my life. Coherent thought fled. The tangy smell of sweat and come and sex permeated the sultry air around me as his hips churned. Salty drops filled my mouth and I lapped them eagerly, using my tongue to stroke his shaft as he pistoned in and out. He didn't ask if I wanted to swallow. He just tightened his painful grip on my hair, shoved his cock deep and shot into my mouth. Come poured down my throat, overflowed past my lips and dribbled down my chin. I sucked and swallowed as fast as I could, drinking in his pungent, briny semen. Nothing existed for me but the sound of his coarse words and the feel of him as he jerked and came.

"Yeah, fuck, oh yeah."

He yanked out of my mouth and shot the last creamy streams across my breasts, the jism dripping off my tingling nipples and onto my thighs as he held my head with one hand and watched himself shoot all over me. He smiled at the come on my lips and chin, his look one of absolute possession.

That look made me crazy. I wanted to wallow in every kinky, raunchy act past lovers had been too squeamish for. I wanted to be thrown down and fucked in every hole until I couldn't move.

The hot wind whipped up abruptly, and the heavens opened in a downpour. He pulled me up and we stood panting beneath the deluge for a moment. Water sluiced off our bodies. I half-expected it to turn to steam as it hit our skin. Instead it mingled with the fluids of sex and ran down our naked flesh. By the time our breathing slowed, we were drenched. When a bolt of lightning struck nearby, he cupped his hand around my neck, grabbed the bottle of tequila and pushed me in front of him, naked, back to my room.

The storm surrounded us and the scent of ozone filled the air. The base, elemental feel of the night was like being in some dark, wicked dream where we reveled in our most animalistic cravings. My body screamed with an atavistic, feral want. I didn't care how he used me, I wanted every moment of pleasure and pain.

He stood in my room, illuminated only by flashes of lightning, swallowing down a third of the remaining tequila. When he shoved the bottle to my lips and held it up, pouring it down my throat, I swallowed until I coughed. He put the bottle on the nightstand.

"On the bed." His command was accompanied by a shove, and I stumbled, fell, crawled eagerly onto the bed on my hands and knees like a bitch in heat.

I could hear him rummaging through my luggage. I had no idea what he was looking for but I panted as I waited impatiently to feel him fill me up again.

I heard the snick of a bottle top, and smelled the incongruously soft aroma of baby oil before he pushed my face down onto the bed. Rough hands slid between the cheeks of my ass, slick oil running over my flesh as his fingers probed.

"So tight. So hot." Thick fingers breached my anus, invading, burning. "I'm going to fuck you up the ass."

"Yes! Yes! Fuck me—fuck my ass!" I begged breathlessly and waited for his penetration. When it came, when he was thrusting deep into my ass, all that was familiar of my life shattered and fell away. As he took me with a ravening brutality I screamed with joy and completion. I screamed over and over again as lightning flashed and my world lit up with a surreal glow.

* * *

I woke up alone the next morning. It was late and the heat of day had already begun to build. It pulsed in the silent stillness of my dingy room. Along with my lover and the magic of the storm, the miasma of lust from the previous night was gone. My body was uncomfortably sore, and I was damp with sweat and sticky body fluids.

Through my tequila-hangover haze I heard the blare of a car horn. I stumbled out of bed taking a second to swish some mouthwash, then grabbed my crumpled suit and pulled it on, ignoring the unmistakable odor of sex and alcohol that wafted off me.

Outside the rental agency driver waited with a new car. He was young, clean-cut and eager. His name was Buddy and he informed me that power had been restored after the storm and they'd received my distress call and located me via GPS. He helped me transfer my luggage and laptop and politely refrained from mentioning my grungy appearance.

Before leaving, I stuck my head into the manager's office. I didn't know what I'd say, but it was empty. There was no sign anyone had been there at all, except for the empty tequila bottles in the trash. The red truck was gone. Only a splotch of oil in the dirt marked where it had been.

I climbed into the car with Buddy while trying to focus on something other than my sore pussy, aching thighs and throbbing breasts. I forced my mind away from the memory of debauched sex acts and tried to think of familiar and unthreatening things. A nice hotel room, a cool shower and clean clothes.

"It's too bad your car didn't make it another twenty miles. There's a decent Motel 6 just down the highway."

"I was lucky to find this place. Better than being stranded on the side of the road."

"Must have been a bit scary though, staying here all by your lonesome during such a big storm, no?"

"Alone? I wasn't alone—the motel manager was there. He gave me a room." And fucked my brains out.

"Manager? Hell, sorry, excuse my French, ma'am, there's no manager here. This motel's been closed since last year. The owner and his wife couldn't make a go of it and moved to Houston."

"But there was a man…"

The driver missed my puzzled response as he twisted the wheel and we bumped sharply onto the highway and pulled away from the motel. I turned in my seat to glance back, and winced as a burning twinge reminded me my ass had been well and thoroughly plundered. Despite the lingering discomfort, the bright light of day made the events of the night before seem distant and unreal. Yet the smell of him remained on my skin, taunting me.

As we drove I spotted a folded newspaper sitting on the dashboard. I could see part of a photograph, a dark-haired man in orange prison garb. I grabbed it and flipped the paper open. The headline read, STILL AT LARGE above Heathcliff's grinning face. The black eyes in the photo were the same riveting ones that had stared into my own as he fucked me.

"Scary dude, huh? He escaped from the Federal Pen three days ago. Feds and the cops haven't found squat. He done, er, did five years of a twenty-year stretch for armed robbery. You're lucky you didn't run into this guy."

I folded the paper and laid it down on the seat. I shut my eyes against the sun blazing through the windshield and asked the driver to turn up the air-conditioning.

As we drove back toward civilization, unsettling thoughts began to infiltrate my mind. Thoughts of quitting my dead-end job and running away. I had no ties. I suddenly ached with a desperate need to escape everything in my life that was unsatisfying, tame and stale. Why not?

The car hummed along and I began to doze and my thoughts grew darker.

Instead of sane and sensible things, I thought of empty motel rooms that smelled of sex. Of blistering heat and summer storms, of wild lightning and unbearable hungers. I thought of a grinning, black-eyed stranger wet and naked in the rain. And I thought of rough, hot hands, a hard cock and screaming out my ecstasy in the freedom of the dark.

TRIPLET TROUBLE

JT Louder

Four years ago, I would have told you that Stephen wasn't my type. I typically like my guys dark—Italian dark, South American dark—but he had light-brown hair, big blue eyes, and rosy red cheeks. Stephen *looked* like a Murphy, so his last name was apt.

There were two other ways he was not my type: he was an engineering major (and had the cell phone belt clip to prove it), and he had absolutely no athletic ability whatsoever. The one and only time we went running together, he somehow managed to bump into me several times, nearly knocking us both off our feet right on the school track.

But even though he wasn't my ideal, in his pursuit of me, he was persistent and kind. He had a great sense of humor, and he sent me texts every day telling me how much he loved me. (He still does.)

And letting him in was a superb idea, especially for my sex life. I spent a good majority of my senior year fucking big, thick-necked jocks in the boys' bathroom or in friends' parents' beds.

They would squeeze my breasts tight like sponges while they rammed their tiny, angry, red-tipped cocks into me, their eyes squeezed shut, teeth clenched into a grimace. It was like, instead of fucking, they were lifting weights after practice.

None of these guys ever made a noise. I had sex in silence for the first two years I was sexually active. They would only grunt when they came—a big, ugly, "Unh!" like they were trying to throw a two-hundred-pound weight across the football field when, actually, they had just shot their load all over my pubic hair and thighs.

I was known as the quiet chick with the nice, tight cunt and a mouth that could make a cock hard as a rock in no time flat. Rumor was that I'd have been a knockout if I was a "screamer." But why fake such extreme pleasure when, first of all, the sex was seldom screaming material, and second, none of those guys urged me on with dirty talk or sexy noises of their own?

Stephen couldn't have been any more different. The first time I sucked his cock, he closed his eyes, tipped his head back, put his hands gently in my hair and moaned so loudly, I thought the girls in the dorm room next to us would know exactly what I was doing, with my roommate having gone home for the long weekend. But I didn't care. I loved how vocal he was, how he'd bite his beautiful, plump lower lip and moan and moan, how he'd thrust his hips gently while I sucked him, letting out a breathy "Yes, yes, yes," how he'd yell, "Oh god, baby! You're fucking making me come!" when he'd shoot off in my mouth.

The first month we were together, we kind of got a reputation on my dorm floor. But I loved that Stephen did what guys expect girls to do—loudly proclaim our ecstasy courtesy of the pump and grind of the Almighty Cock, roll our heads from side to side like we could barely take another inch of it and pant and whine like oversexed sex kittens. And I loved that he didn't expect a thing in return, although I gave it to him. How could I not moan wildly when my guy was crying my name, his nipples hard and eyes closed like a sleeping angel's, his short, thick cock widening my pussy with every pump of his slender hips?

But here was the best part: Stephen was a triplet.

Yes, I was the one who brought it up. Yes, he was shocked at first, but when I wrapped my arms around him as we snuggled in my twin bed, his come drying in some bunched-up tissues to my right, he slowly warmed to the idea.

"You'd want all three of us?" he asked, soft and curious, like a young boy.

I said, "You're all identical, right?"

He contemplated this for a while, finally giving a tiny shrug. "Yeah, pretty much."

I pressed my lips into the soft brown hair near his temple. "How could I not want to play with two other versions of you?"

He let out a gentle laugh and gave my nipple a quick tweak, rolling me over onto my back. I felt his cock begin to harden against my leg as he lowered his forehead to touch mine. He said, "Let me make a few phone calls then."

Before Thanksgiving break, he asked me to marry him. I said yes—how could I not say yes to a lifetime of "Oh, oh, I fucking love your pussy! I fucking love your pussy!" I told him that it would be a long engagement—after we graduated in the spring, I was committed to studying architecture in Paris. I wanted to start my life before I committed to a husband.

I went home with Stephen for the first two weeks of our semester break to spend Christmas with his family, to meet his mom and dad, and those two identical brothers. Stephen drove his truck slowly over snow-packed roads, the storm having tapered off then, as he put his hand on my knee and said, "This weekend, I will give you the best gift of your life."

I fidgeted with my diamond ring. "What could possibly be left?"

He smiled wide, his cheeks pinker than usual from the cold. "I have it all planned. Just wait."

And he did. Down to the minute, maybe the second—who knows. We were the first to arrive at his family's winter home in Vermont, one that looked nestled into the side of a big, snow-covered mountain when we pulled in from the narrow road.

We took the opportunity to shower together, rinsing away our three-and-a-half-hour drive. I washed his hair and he washed mine. I soaped his cock and he soaped my pussy, then reached farther to tease my asshole with a slippery finger as I sucked on his gorgeous lips. All I remember is the heat from the shower and the heat from his body and the heat of his breath in my ear, and for a little while, all I could think was, "Okay, maybe we can marry this June."

We were hot and heavy even before we ended up naked on the sofa, me in his lap, a loud, slapping noise from my skin meeting his while I rode up and down on this thick cock, and he was crying, "Fuck, fuck yes! Take me deep, baby!" His wide piece had just hit my spot and I was letting out my own wail of an orgasm when I felt the blast of cold air, opened my eyes, and saw them.

There were two other Stephens standing in the doorway, big duffle bags on their shoulders: one Stephen aghast, his mouth open and eyes wide, and the other with his blue eyes narrowed, a small smirk on his face. This Stephen instantly reminded me of the jocks I used to fuck when I was younger.

I don't know why I didn't feel the need to cover up or run into a bedroom from sheer embarrassment. I let Stephen lift me off his lap, his cock standing straight out when he stood, and said, "Brothers, you're right on time." I remember thinking, *"Brothers" sounds strangely cultish, and what religion was he raised in again?* Stephen continued. "Sonja, these are my brothers Jack"—the jock Stephen—"and Tommy"—the tinier, nerdier, freaked-out Stephen with wire-rimmed glasses like Harry Potter's. "Guys," Stephen said. "This is Sonja, my wife-to-be."

It felt strange to not say a word, with me sitting on the couch completely naked and still flushed from coming. So what I muttered was, "Nice to meet you both."

Jack hadn't lifted his gaze from my tits, still wearing his creepy smirk. I would keep him straight in my head by secretly referring to him as "Jackass," which, as of that moment, seemed more than appropriate. Another option: Jack-Off, a nickname that was timely, considering the bulge in his pants.

Jack-Off dropped his bag to the floor, unzipped his coat, and stepped out of his snow boots. Tommy shut the front door behind him, clenching the strap of his backpack with one, white-knuckled hand. I watched as my Stephen gave his cock a little tug, ensuring its hardness, wanting to be ready.

Jack hung his coat on one of the hooks on the wall, and then joined us near the sofa. Seeing him stand next to Stephen was surreal. They were identical in height and build. It looked like neither of them had shaved that morning, so even the stubble on their faces appeared to be of identical length. The only thing that set them apart was Jack's creepy, predatory stare versus the always soft and warm expression of my Stephen. Jack finally lifted his eyes to meet mine. "It's nice to finally meet you, Sonja. We've heard so much." He paused, and then, "So, you up for some triplet trouble tonight?"

Oh, Jack-Off, you corny jackass. His smile wasn't exactly

unfriendly, but it made me question, although only for a second, this idea of mine to take on all three of the Murphy boys.

I looked back to Tommy, who was still standing at the front door in his big, puffy ski jacket zipped high to his chin and his matching red hat with white pom-pom. I felt warm hands on my shoulders and knew they were Stephen's. With my eyes still on Tommy, Stephen said softly into my ear, "If it's okay with you, honey, we'd like Tommy to be the star of this show. He's still a virgin—."

"That probably doesn't surprise you much," Jack interrupted.

Stephen continued, "—and I can't think of a better or more delicious woman than you to take it from him." Stephen brushed his fingers along the base of my neck, sending the most amazing shivers throughout my body and hardening my nipples. I thought, *If all three of you can touch me like that, then let's get this show started.*

"And we," Jack said, "as his brothers, will be here to support him." He unbuckled his belt and pulled his sweatshirt over his head, revealing a chest as smooth as my Stephen's, but with sinewy muscles in his arms and stomach.

I said to Tommy, "Does that sound good to you, sweetheart?" I tried to make it sound sexy, not matronly.

From behind me, Stephen said, "You don't call me sweetheart," and Jack let out a gruff chuckle.

Tommy pressed his glasses back on his nose. "I think so. Yeah."

There was something incredible about this smaller, more timid version of my Stephen, and suddenly, there was nothing I wanted more than to see Tommy where his brother had been: naked beneath me as I rode his hard cock.

I moved from the couch and made my way, naked, to Tommy.

Holding his even gaze, I took the hat from his head and pulled the bag from his shoulder, nearly dropping it to the floor from its heavy weight. Tommy smiled then, and I could feel my pussy tinge—a sign of me getting wetter. I pressed my body against the front of his puffy coat, its coolness shocking my hot skin, and brought him in for the softest closed-mouth kiss I've ever given or received. Taking both his hands in mine, I said, "Come join us on the couch."

"Fuck, yeah!" Who else could that be? No one but Jack. He sounded like my Stephen, but Jack was louder, which matched his energy and swagger. When I turned back toward them, they both had their hard cocks in their hands. Stephen gave his a slow, long rub, his eyes dreamy on me, while Jack worked his piece quick and hard like he was seconds from shooting his load all over the red Pottery Barn sofa. (New nickname, perhaps: "Jack Rabbit.") I noticed that Jack's dick was far thinner and just slightly longer than Stephen's. *Typical*, I thought, that the douche bag of the three would have the tiniest cock.

And then I thought that this boded well for Tommy, who was following me as he stripped off his coat, stopping for a moment to balance unsteadily on one foot and slip off a snow boot. When I sat back on the sofa, I reached out and ran my nails along the underside of Stephen's tight balls while he stroked that thick cock I loved so much.

He bent over to kiss me ardently, his tongue forceful against my own, and it was just what I needed. This hot kiss was his continued consent, his encouragement for me to fuck his virgin brother while he and Jack did whatever it was they would do, and that didn't matter, because Stephen was there and Stephen was hard and Stephen, I felt, would keep us all safe in the end.

When my lips broke from his, Stephen put two fingers in his mouth before he pushed them into my wet cunt. I gasped, spreading my legs farther apart to urge on a good cockless fucking. He smiled at my response, but moved his fingers from my hole. "That's my girl," he said.

"Holy shit—" It was Jackass who grabbed our attention, and when we turned to look, it all made sense. Tommy—thinner, bonier and whiter skinned than his two brothers—stood tall with his enormous cock jutting out from a thick bush of brown pubic hair. I didn't even notice his balls (which were proportionate, I guess, but not ugly—just *big*) because my head was swimming with numbers: Seven inches? Eight inches? More? How big was this boy's cock? It was not only long, but thick like my Stephen's, and before I even started to worry about where exactly I was supposed to fit all of it, I heard Stephen say, "Yeah. I'll get the lube."

Jack said, a little too aggressively, "Dude, why didn't you *tell* me your cock was that *big*?"

Before a wince took over Tommy's face completely, I grabbed his hand and brought him down to the couch with me. I looked up at Jack. "It's a surprise, right?" Then I looked at Tommy. "It's a very, very nice surprise. Sit back against the cushions, okay, sweetheart?"

Stephen returned. "Here," he said, and I opened my hand flat for him. "A condom and some lube."

I tucked the tiny bottle of lubricant into my free hand and offered Tommy the condom with the other. "Do you want to put this on, or should I?"

There was a quiver in his lips that I promised myself I would kiss away when his cock was thrusting deep inside my pussy, filling me far more than his brother ever would.

"You can," Tommy said. We both looked down at his cock, big and hard and wet at the tip.

I slipped the condom on and squeezed some lube onto my

fingers, rubbing it first into my already wet hole, and then applying more to Tommy's length. I heard my Stephen moan while he watched us, and, somewhat surprisingly, Jack joined in, just as loud as his brother, if not louder. I loved knowing that they were behind us, the two jerking their cocks in completely different, non-identical ways—the Jack Rabbit to my right, my slow-and-steady boy on my left.

I straddled Tommy, bringing my tits so close to his face that I grazed his lips with a hard nipple. I said, "Hold your cock for me," and Tommy gave a little nod, looking down again into his lap. I lowered myself slowly, feeling the wide head of his cock against my slit, and then lower again, taking him with only a little difficulty, with many thanks to the lube and that amazing kiss and quick finger-fuck from my Stephen. I pressed down until I couldn't take any more of Tommy, feeling full and stretched. I held perfectly still until I felt *full* and *stretched*—in a far sexier sense now, in a way that I knew meant I could take him, that I could move my hips, bounce up and down on Tommy's cock, and hope he wasn't too much that I wouldn't be able to come. I wanted so desperately to give him my orgasm, my tiny, nerdy, soon-to-be brother-in-law. I wanted Jack to be envious, and I wanted Stephen to be proud.

Speaking of the devils, I could hear their moans grow louder. My Stephen said, "Let me see it, baby. Let me see him inside you."

Again, I leaned forward into Tommy, my tits in his face, and used my hands to spread the cheeks of my ass so the guys could take a look at how wide Tommy's cock stretched my slit. This time, Tommy took advantage, flicking his tongue over my nipple.

I started to move slowly up and down on Tommy's cock. I turned my head first toward Jack, then toward Stephen, snapping both my fingers. "Both of you—stand here on the couch next to us. I want to see those cocks."

When they joined us, I fell back onto Tommy's cock courtesy of all the jostling, and we both gasped. I looked down onto Tommy's smile, watched as he closed his eyes and lowered his head back on the cushion of the sofa—a position I'd seen his brother in hundreds of times before. With Stephen's and Jack's cocks at eye level on either side of me, I took a gentle hold of them both, moving my hips again up and down on Tommy's hardness. While I fucked him, I worked my hand gently over the length of Jack's hard cock, and brought Stephen's to my mouth, licking the head and tugging the way I knew he liked.

Soon, it was a moan fest. Stephen—my beautiful Stephen— had his hands on his hips, which he rocked forward, urging me to take his cock into my mouth, and how could I refuse his shameless noises, his "Suck it, baby. Fuck him, yeah." Jack's moans were higher in pitch, bordering on sounding like a boy's whimper. *Jackie*, I thought then. *Little Jackie.* His strange, young noises were something I never knew would turn me on as much as they did. Because of those noises, I left Stephen only with the attention of my hand moving on his thick, wet piece, but at least he had the pleasure of watching me take as much as I could of Jack's smaller cock down my throat. The more I took, the higher and louder Jack's moans grew, and that spurred on my Stephen, who was moaning, "Oh, oh, oh," and Tommy finally chimed in, saying, "Fuck, fuck, fuck, this is so fucking good," as I rode him at a furious pace. It was his hot skin now that was slapping against my own with every bounce, having taken the place of his brother beneath me on the couch.

Okay. I was surrounded by three guys—triplets—who were the most vocal men I'd ever been with, and fuck you, bad porn, and fuck you, shitty high school boyfriends: guys can be—what would you call it: vulnerable? emotional? acknowledging?— enough to open their mouths and use their vocal chords for something other than an occasional grunt. I felt like my body and hands and mouth were conducting a symphony, with Stephen's loud "Work my cock hard with that hand, baby!" and Jack's loud, high-pitched moans, followed by the occasional "Fuck, you're so good!" and Tommy's "Damn, your pussy's so wet and hot!" With music so beautiful, how could I not move my mouth from Jack's cock and scream out my own orgasm, louder than the three brothers, the final crescendo, as my Stephen groaned, matching my volume, and shot his huge, creamy load across my tits. This brought on Jack's orgasm, his little-boy squeals coming loud and fast, growing higher in pitch all the while, as I worked him with my hand. Jack wasn't a shooter, but more of an erupter. I watched as his clear come dripped from the head of his cock onto my hand and some onto the couch, his eyes closed and lips luscious and pouty like my Stephen's.

Tommy was thrusting up into me, and I took him with such ease, I could only imagine the state in which he would leave my cunt. Would I ever be tight enough for Stephen again? It didn't matter. Tommy's orgasm was louder than Stephen's and deeper than Jack's, and when he thrust far inside me for the final time, he yelled, "Sonja! Sonja! Oh, fuck!" like I was tearing him to pieces, like he'd never make it out of this orgasm alive, with his wire-rimmed glasses low and lopsided on his nose. Tommy was a sound and vision—and with his cock buried in me, a total sensory experience. It was sexy enough to coax my pussy into clenching again as he made me come a second time.

It was the only time we did it—two days before Christmas during our final year of college. Stephen and I married two years later, and at our wedding, I danced closely with both of his brothers. My favorite picture from our big day is the one where the photographer encouraged the three brothers to surround me, and you can see each of their hands on my body, and my smile is wide and electric.

THE UNREQUITED ORGASM

Dani Bauter

Tonight it took me not one, not two, but three times to get off. I was starting to feel a little guilty about not giving my lover any rest; I had to leave him with a little lotion in his bottle for later, when it was his wife's turn. Nevertheless I climbed on his lap and whispered my request for a fourth, a record for me. Since I'd offered to do all the work, my lover didn't refuse. I gave him my specialty, a lap dance I'd been perfecting after I visited that strip club with my coworkers at lunchtime a few weeks ago. Those women inspired me, made me want to tease my lover with the way that my body moved. I took off every single piece of clothing and moved my hips to the conga beat of the music, rocking on him. I watched as he shut his eyes and moaned deep, at the back of his throat. I kissed him and he grabbed my breasts. I rubbed myself on his cock and felt it grow against my thighs.

I wasn't focusing on anything right now but our passion, the little earthquakes and volcanoes that erupt within me whenever I'm around him. Even though we had only recently met

I couldn't imagine him being very far away, and sometimes the thought scared me. We fucked with an urgency and intensity that blew both of us away. We told each other our most intimate desires and embarrassing secrets, and always ended our evening with a little fooling around and guaranteed mind-blowing orgasms. Then we went our separate ways, him back to his wife who he didn't love—not that he could love anyone. I became more and more confused every day but I tried to focus on the present moment, because that seemed to always get me through. That was, until I met Lina, the second half of Hollywood's power couple.

She came to me as if in a dream, those huge, beautiful gray eyes and lips that begged to be kissed. I had never felt that way about women before, and Lina was clearly an exception. She had come to visit me because she had found my business card in her husband's wallet, and wanted to find out just exactly what services I was providing for him. But when our eyes met for the first time there was something more than charged civility conducting between us. Fortunately I had the proper credentials—as a journalist I had interviewed her husband about his role in his latest movie, among other things. Business aside, I invited my guest to stay for a drink, perhaps a glass of red wine? Lina accepted.

Instead of being an adoring fan, I started talking about myself, sharing details of my life with Lina that I had never told anyone before. Of course, I neglected to mention the extent of the services I was providing for her husband. Lina had this silent way about her that intrigued me—I could tell she was really listening, and considering the things that I was telling her. Her eyes revealed that. Lina's pout was a different story. Soon I got lost in the sound of my own voice and Lina's gaze.

Hours passed before either of us realized what time it was.

Lina was late for a meeting with her agent, and I had to get started on a story I was writing. "I had a great time, we should do this again sometime," Lina murmured, with a smirk that both bothered and aroused me.

"We will," I replied, all traces of doubt purposefully absent from my voice.

The two of us went back to our separate lives. I continued to see Brady in private, one time even at their house. Surrounded by photos of the two of them, I couldn't help but check out the ones of Lina. What was it about her that made me so horny? It was like her eyes spoke to me, connected with me in a way no one had ever done before. Brady even noticed.

"Lucy. Are you there, sweetie?" Brady was getting more and more annoyed with me because sometimes it took him a while to get my attention, so hung up was I on that photo of Lina in the leather pants, long hair covering her breasts, a black panther on a leash next to her. I was creaming my jeans and I couldn't figure out why. And then I started to ask questions, which really bugged Brady.

"What is Lina like in bed?" I was once so bold to ask, and Brady stopped in the middle of our fucking, put his shorts on, and went downstairs to get a glass of orange juice. I really didn't think it was going to bother him that much. Being a woman, I'd had the notion of a threesome with another woman proposed to me more than once. But apparently I'd overlooked that one huge item—the male ego.

Eventually after enough of the questions, Brady got fed up with me and shouted his disgust. I started thinking about how things had become ugly between us. That we might as well quit now while we were ahead and try to maintain a healthy friendship. Hot sex aside, Brady was attempting to control me, and I didn't like it. I finally confronted him one night after he'd talked about not remembering the last time he'd had sex with his wife. I mused for a couple of too-short moments about how I'd make every second count with her, and then used the comment as an opportunity to segue into my need to just be his friend. I told him that my friendship was the most I could offer him, that what we were doing was wrong and how he could never give me everything I want and need.

"Curious how women always have this 'all or nothing' attitude," he commented. It didn't matter what kind of remark he made or even how he responded, I was glad I'd gotten the words out and silently congratulated myself for being honest with my heart. I left shortly after that, and when I got home there was a message on my machine from Lina, telling me I could call her back on her cell phone if I liked. I liked. I called her back before I even hung up my coat, and we picked up right where we had left off a couple of weeks before. It was her turn to invite me to a bar down the street from where she and Brady lived. We agreed to meet in an hour, so I set off to find the perfect outfit. Not that I was trying to impress her or anything.

An hour later we sat down and ordered our drinks—a mojito for me and a Pacifico for her. There was a butchness about her that was beginning to turn me on. Lina opened up a bit more this time, telling me about the significance of each of her tattoos—there were more than a dozen of them. I told her about some of the characters I'd come across during my time spent as a journalist, and she helped to fill in some of the blanks that just didn't make sense until I had her insight. I didn't even realize when my hand had reached out and rested on her thigh, and she didn't push it away either. Instead she gazed at me with that insanely intense stare, and we had another conversation of the nonverbal variety. A couple of hours and a couple of drinks later, we decided that it was time to find our way home while we still remembered where home was.

I left Lina at my door, thinking about her lips the whole time and wondering what they would feel like pressed against mine. I wanted to part them with my tongue and find hers, my hands full of her hair and her fingers squeezing my nipples. Unfortunately Lina had more class than that. She bent over quickly and gave me a kiss on the lips, but it was one of those kisses that could be construed as a friendly peck. And that's what it probably was. But she did say that she had a great time, and we should do it again sometime. A startling moment of déjà vu was replaced with dim hope.

Apparently rejection is some kind of aphrodisiac because when I got inside my voice mail was filled with messages from Brady, checking in on me and wanting to know where I was. I wondered why Lina had felt the need to hide our meeting from him. Nonetheless, I picked up the phone and dialed their number so that I could tell Brady just exactly why he didn't need to bother wondering. I figured if Lina picked up I would say I was calling to tell her I'd had a great time, or something cheesy like that. I was sure she'd eat it up.

"Hello?" Brady answered, sounding a little exasperated.

"Brady? Hey, it's Lucy. I wanted to call you back and tell you—"

"We're going to have to talk later." Brady cut me off before I even had a chance to finish.

"Okay, whatever," I replied, to a dead line.

I went to bed shortly after that, and was just drifting off to sleep when the phone rang. Figuring it was Brady calling me back, I answered the phone on the first ring.

"Hi, what are you doing calling my husband at this hour? Who the hell are you?" A familiar female voice filled my ears, and I heard another voice, a male one, laughing in the background. I knew that I couldn't hang up because if she called back again and got my voice mail she'd know it was me, so I tried to disguise my voice and tell her I had called the wrong number earlier. She didn't buy it; she recognized my voice right away.

"Lucy, why are you lying to me?" The hurt in her voice made me shudder, and I couldn't say a word. "It's what I think it is, isn't it? It's what I suspected. Brady really is fooling around on me. But I forgot the icing on the cake—it's with you. Fuck that, I'll be right over."

"Lina, what? What are you talking about? Why don't we just sleep on this and talk about it tomorrow, when we've both got a clear mind?"

"No. We're going to talk about this now." Lina was dead serious and sounded, frankly, like she might blow at any second. I had no choice but to agree. Twenty minutes later she was knocking at my door, and it was clear by the tone that her anger hadn't cooled off yet. I answered it in my black silk robe and nothing underneath, hoping that she'd see it as a symbol of surrender.

She went off as soon as she stepped inside the threshold, asking me who the hell I thought I was, fooling around with her husband and then using her. "Wait a second, using you? I cut your husband loose and this is the thanks I get? I thought I was interested in pursuing you; at least that's what my clit's been telling me lately."

"Wait, what?" This time Lina couldn't hide her surprise, not that she ever could. But then she finally looked, really looked, at me—let her eyes take in the silk and the curves and my long, dark curly hair. And she licked her lips and smirked. The smirk that had aroused and bothered me before, now just aroused me. She reached out, untied my robe and helped me shrug out of it, letting it fall to the floor. Lina squeezed my nipples just like in my fantasy as she leaned in to kiss me. When our tongues touched, the tiniest bit of wetness dribbled down my thigh.

I decided that she had too many clothes on, so we took them off as quickly as possible. We fell to the floor in front of the fireplace. Soon my legs were wrapped around her waist, our breasts pressed together so hard that it felt like we were molding into one. My clit was getting harder and I began rubbing it against her stomach, getting more and more lubricated with each pass up and down. But suddenly Lina pulled away. She looked deep into my eyes and shook her head.

"No. What you did was wrong. And you need to be punished for your actions." She raised her hand and pulled it back, but I didn't see it until it was too late because I was too into stroking my clit against her tummy.

Smack! Lina brought her hand down onto my tush so hard it stung. But it also made me wetter, a moan escaping from my lips unintentionally. She probably didn't know how to take this, but I knew how I needed to take it. I raised my ass higher, a silent plea to punish me again. *Smack! Smack!* Lina gave me a double shot this time, and I felt myself get extra gooey.

"I want you to lie in front of me like a bad girl." Lina coaxed me onto my side next to her, my back to her, my ass ready to get stroked, smacked, and spanked. "You gotta learn your lesson," she murmured, her voice catching in her throat, probably because my moans were even beginning to turn me on. Not that I needed much help in that department.

"Dip your finger in here," I instructed Lina, showing her what I meant with my own finger. When my fingertip made contact with my clit, I knew I wasn't going to be able to last much longer.

"Wait, I got something." Lina paused for a second to reach in her bag, pulling out a strap-on harness and dildo. This woman obviously packed for many occasions. She put it on with the swiftness of someone who had some practice, and my cunt glistened with appreciation. The dildo itself was huge, bigger than any man I'd ever fucked, that was for sure. And the thought that it was never going to go soft, that I could ride it forever if I wanted, almost sent me over the top.

Instead I flipped Lina over and climbed on, riding her just like I had her husband during a time that seemed like ages ago at that moment. I used my abnormally strong thighs to maneuver the dildo's base over Lina's clit while I focused the other end on my G-spot. She used my nipples to guide her on our ride. "You feel so good inside me," I told her, ready to let go any second. She was enjoying her own ecstasy below me, her teeth biting her lip and her eyes rolling to the back of her head. I came collapsing on top of her, my tongue and teeth caressing her neck while she dug her nails into my back. Her breathing lulled us both to sleep.

We awoke a while later and she went home. Even with her hair all mussed and her makeup smeared, she was still so beautiful to me. I hoped she would give me some sign that she wanted to see me again, like she had before. Instead she said nothing, and her hug seemed a little detached when we said good-bye. I told myself I was imagining things and went into the kitchen to make some coffee and eat breakfast. I wondered about her equipment: why had she brought it with her last night? I almost choked on my bagel as I realized that she had done all this lesbian stuff before.

And then I sat down to start writing my next article.

THE DANCER

Evey Brett

It's the magazine photograph that captures Lauren's attention, that sleek dancer's body bare-chested and bent backward onto the stage, arms outstretched, leggings leaving nothing to the imagination.

Rafael Escalante, the caption says, but her attention is riveted on that fine build with every muscle standing out in stark perfection. His eyes are closed as if he's dreaming...or submitting.

That thought sets her imagination afire. She runs the scissors down the center of the magazine and carefully extracts the picture. She shoves aside the picture of her dear husband, Edward—may he rest in peace—and replaces it with Rafael's. For a while she's lost in a daydream in which he's lying on the bed beneath her, willing to submit to whatever she wishes to do. He moans when she pinches his nipples and shudders when she reaches between his legs and grasps his balls through the fabric. That look of fierce concentration never leaves his face as she explores his body with her mouth and leaves a trail of kisses, ending just before she reaches his erection.

She doesn't touch that. Not yet. She teases him instead. She strokes his inner thighs and watches him squirm while she comes near to, but not quite touching, his cock.

And when she draws the leggings down, he's like a merman, legs trapped together and flailing helplessly. At last she puts her mouth on that fine, uncut cock and sucks him, listening to him whimper and moan in pleasure. His balls tighten and he comes in a thick, salty burst, and her mouth fills with the taste of him.

Later, she reads the article accompanying the picture. Rafael grew up in the slums of Buenos Aires and earned a few coins dancing for the tourists. One of them noticed his talent, and with great effort, arranged for him to study in the United States, where he eventually became a modern dance star with his own troupe. In the past year he's nearly lost everything. He broke his ankle mid-tour and had to cancel shows. His dancers left to find more profitable work. His patron passed away and in the resulting tussle over the estate, all of Rafael's funding had been withdrawn. He's desperately in need of support.

How convenient she's in the position to provide it.

Lauren's husband—dear Edward—had been the head of a software firm that made it big in the nineties. After he died in a boating accident, she'd done her best to run the company until the responsibilities grew too great for her to handle. She remains on the board and occasionally acts as consultant, but the company is now in the hands of a younger, more excited generation, leaving her free to engage in more philanthropic pursuits.

Rafael, she knows, will be one such pursuit. Dear Edward wouldn't be shocked by her fantasies. He was quite aware that he was a comely man who cared more for intellectual pursuits than physical, so he never denied her the occasional night away from home. Neither would he begrudge her setting up a fund to aid Rafael, which she does. Promptly.

She scours Internet articles and dance magazines, tracking Rafael's career as best as she can. Her bedroom wall soon resembles a teenager's, since she cut out or printed every picture of him she found. There are headshots, photos of him in the air with his legs extended in a leap, and one where he's standing behind a woman, his hands roving sensually over her body. They're both dressed in faux furs that cover the bare minimum, as if they're creatures just emerging from the jungle and engage in little more than carnal pursuits.

She imagines she's that woman, onstage, with his arms wrapped around her waist. His cock juts hard between her legs and she rubs her ass against it. He moans softly into her ear as he grabs her breasts and tears the covering away, baring her to the chilly air.

She guides his hand lower, down the curve of her belly and beneath the tiny fur skirt. She's already wet and throbbing with anticipation. He's cautious, making no move until she urges him to. She pushes his fingers inward until he slips one, then two inside her and she's riding his hand, fucking his fingers. He shudders and thrusts forward and his hardness is between her legs. He smells like a wild thing, sweaty and green. His rough cheek scrapes hers, leaving scratches, but she doesn't care.

Together they slick his cock and her asshole. Then he wraps his free arm around her ribs for support and thrusts again. The entry burns. She gasps, but the discomfort is soon replaced by the welcome tingling of having something so hot and thick buried to the hilt inside her. His fingers continue to rub so she's being fucked twice over. They're both breathing hard, and his cock makes wet, sucking sounds as he plunges it into her body. They're both wild creatures, mindless in their passion. She screams when she comes, like the feral thing she is.

Rafael wants to start an organization designed to teach low-income or refugee children how to dance. She thinks it's a wonderful idea and helps organize a gala and auction for his benefit. As part of the celebration, he puts on a performance. Part of it showcases the talent of his young stars, boys and girls of all races together onstage and moving their bodies with fiery abandon.

The other part is a solo by Rafael, a soft, sensual dance in which he expresses both the passion for his homeland and the hardships he's gone through to become what he is. She watches everything over the Internet, tears in her eyes. She wants desperately to attend, but her latest surgery leaves her trapped in her bedroom.

Her consolation prize arrives in the mail a week later. She'd bid so high on one of Rafael's costumes, a black jacket with gold trim, that no one else could approach her. She holds it to her nose and breathes in. It smells like sweat. *His* sweat.

She has a picture of him wearing that jacket when he portrayed the title role in *The Sleeping Prince*. It's a twisted, erotic version of *Sleeping Beauty* set to the Argentine tango music of Astor Piazzolla. The prince falls prey to a spell and is discovered by a princess so warped after being raised by a dragon she intends to devour him, body and soul. Sex wakens him, and he's so transfixed by her attentions that he doesn't beg for his life. Fascinated by his reaction, she keeps him captive for forty years, until he dies of old age, still madly in love and unfazed by his treatment.

One of her assistants has tracked down a recording of his

performance. With the jacket in her arms she watches it again and again, utterly absorbed by the way he gives himself to his partner without once sacrificing his masculinity.

The jacket lies on the bed beside her and she imagines him there, wearing it. She fingers the jeweled flaps and works the buttons open, baring his chest, inhaling the scent of his masculinity.

There is no sex this time. Instead, he holds her in his tender grasp, body warm against hers and banishing the pain in her back and legs.

In real life, she has to rely on the morphine.

It takes a few months, but at long last, Rafael brings his troupe to San Diego. It's at the tail end of a continental tour that has met with great success and acclaim. She couldn't be prouder of all the good reviews and sold-out audiences.

With her assistant's help, she dons a dress for the first time in nearly two years. She puts her hair up and wears the diamond necklace and earrings dear Edward gave her for her birthday. A private box is hers for the duration of the show so Rafael won't see her. No one will, and it's for the best.

His performances take her breath away. In her mind she's onstage with him, in his arms, alternately thrusting him away and drawing him close. Their bodies move together, dancing and leaping to the music. She runs her fingers over his shoulders, down his long, muscled arms, and runs his hand down her cheek.

When the applause starts, she has just enough self-awareness left to toss her bouquet onto the stage at his feet. She's taped a note to the roses with her name and instructions to visit her box after the final performance.

She knows he will come. She must have him, and soon.

* * *

On the last night, still breathless from the endless rounds of applause, Lauren's sitting in the hard-backed tapestry chair when he arrives. He's not as tall as she might have thought. It's his presence that gives him a height and size that seem to extend beyond the limitations of the stage. Yet here in the seclusion and semidarkness he's small and shy and she loves him just the same. His skin glistens from sweat, and he wears a pair of leggings and a black silk robe tied loosely around his waist. "*Señora* Talbot?"

She holds out her hands, too stunned by his nearness to speak. He takes them and bends down to kiss each, eliciting an almost electric shock. She hadn't expected to have so visceral a reaction.

"It is a pleasure to meet you at last." He kneels on one knee like a knight before his lady, clasping her hands. "My gratitude knows no bounds. I have been able to aid so many people because of your gifts."

The words are lovely, but his body even more so. She can't help staring at him, at the expanse of bare chest peeking through his robe. It's easy to imagine running her fingers over his firm flesh. She has half a mind to seduce him here and now and let the sounds of their lovemaking echo in the empty theater. "You're even more beautiful in person." She squeezes his fingers, committing the sensation to memory.

He smiles. "So are you, *señora.* I trust you enjoyed the performance?"

"I love watching you." She disentangles her hand and boldly runs it through his sweat-dampened hair. It's thick and coarse and she's tempted to yank his head back and lick the salt from his aquiline throat. "I don't mean to keep you. I'm sure you must have a get-together with your dancers."

"Not tonight. We leave for South America early in the morning. Everyone is either packing or sleeping."

"Except you."

"Except me." Instead of taking the other chair, he sits on the floor, stretching his legs and leaning against hers. "You should have told me earlier you were here. I would have thanked you in front of the audience."

She's flattered and tells him so. "Mentioning the foundation in the program is plenty."

"But you deserve to have your moment onstage." He extends his hands behind him and bends backward in a stretch. Then, to her dismay, he drags her crutches into sight. "Are you afraid to be seen because of these?"

It's hard to say which is more upsetting, that he knows her secret or that he's accusing her of cowardice. "I'm not afraid. It's simply better if I stay behind the scenes." This is the moment she's feared, that Rafael, so comfortable with his perfect body, would be repulsed by her scarred and broken one.

But his voice is compassionate rather than condescending. "Better for whom?"

Angry, she gestures for him to give her the crutches, but he holds them just out of reach.

"*Señora* Lauren Talbot. Wife of the late Edward Talbot, who drowned in a boating accident almost two years ago. The boat hit a rock. You were slammed against the railing and sustained nearly two-dozen fractures and broken bones. Except for various philanthropic projects, you've kept out of sight. I had a suspicion as to why."

She keeps her head down, unwilling to see his expression, but he places a hand on her knee. The heat and energy in his touch reach straight to her core and she's dizzy with wanting him.

"Look, *señora.*"

She does. In her lap he's set a photograph. Shock radiates through her body. She claps a hand to her mouth. It's the picture dear Edward took a week before he died. It's her, brown hair loose in the ocean air. Her head is tilted to the side and she's wearing a coy, come-hither expression as she sits on the prow of their catamaran. The media grabbed that picture and used it for their headlines. For over a year she's hated it, seeing it as a reminder of what she'd once been and was no more, but Rafael's hand is trembling.

He slides the photo back into his pocket. "When my last patron died, a part of me died as well. I thought I had lost everything, but then I saw your face in the news and thought, *This woman, she has lost more. I still have my body. I can dance. Her strength will carry me forward, and one day, one day I will have a chance to thank her.* That was before you donated money to me."

Tremors rack her body. Her heart is breaking now that she knows her trials have inspired Rafael just as his did her. It would have been so much safer to keep him at a distance and let him remain in her fantasies. "I'm not afraid of being onstage."

"Prove it." He holds out her crutches.

She feels his gaze on her as she slips her arms into the cuffs and hauls herself to her feet. Glaring at him in challenge, she heads to the door. Step by awkward step she makes her way down the hallway to the elevator, which she takes to the first floor. More than once, she thinks Rafael will get bored and leave her behind, but he doesn't. Instead, he watches her, not with the pity she'd feared, but the way a teacher judges his student.

"This way," he says, and leads her to the backstage door. He holds it open for her, and in an instant she enters another world. At first it's only the overhead fluorescents providing illumination, but Rafael disappears and the side lights flare to life. A moment later, the thick red curtain lifts into the air and she's dazzled by the spots shining on her.

Blinded, she nearly misses Rafael running across the stage and leaping into the air. Nimbly he lands at her side, going down on one knee and spreading his hands wide to encompass the entire theater. "Welcome to my playground, *señora.*"

She gazes down at him, utterly entranced by his naked upper body and his pose of pleading submission. Unable to resist, she clasps his face and bends down and kisses him on the forehead.

He surges to his feet and they're close, so close. She leans against the warm firmness of his body and lets out a long, shuddering sigh. He embraces her and lets out a ragged breath of his own. "Tell me how I can repay you for your kindness." He places her hand against his chest.

It's all the invitation she needs. Her belly, so used to pain instead of pleasure, throbs with the ache of desire. "Dance with me, Rafael."

"We need some music." He winks at her. "I told the security man I had a rehearsal. A private one."

She likes the sound of that. Once more he disappears, leaving her alone and sorely missing his touch. The she hears the faint strains of violin and piano, joined by contrabass, guitar and finally bandoneon. It's Astor Piazzolla's music, which means Rafael has one particular dance in mind.

Her suspicion is confirmed when he slides a chaise longue onto the stage. It's covered in cushioned red velvet and perfect for reclining and sleeping.

In a courtly gesture, he holds out his hand. "You know this piece, I believe?"

She clasps his fingers and nods, having watched *The Sleeping*

Prince hundreds of times but never once believing she'd play the princess.

"You won't need these." He disentangles her hands from the crutches and slides them beside the chaise longue, out of the way. Then he stretches out on the chaise longue and tugs her down beside him.

It's just as she'd dreamed. She can't perform the fancy movements Rafael's usual partner does, but it doesn't matter. For this time and space, he's her prince, and she can play with him how she likes. The music, appropriately titled *"Resurrección del Ángel,"* is calm and thoughtful as she runs her hands along his skin. A tingle of anticipation gathers low in her belly. His nipples are a dark nut brown. She fingers them then traces an invisible line to his belly button.

The rule is that he won't wake until she kisses him, so she takes her time. She already knows every inch of his body, having studied it from every angle, but touching it is like magic. She pries his thighs apart and cups his cock through the thin black leggings. It's hot and already hard. A shiver rolls through his body at her touch.

The music picks up. Her dress is suddenly stifling and too tight so she reaches behind for the zipper and shrugs it off until she's wearing only her slip, panties and bra. Her legs, thin, twisted and no longer made for dancing, are still covered.

Timing it perfectly with the music, she leaves a trail of kisses up his neck and, as the piece reaches its climax, presses her lips to his. His eyes open slowly, taking in her partially clad form, and from his deep groan she knows he's not acting.

The music changes to *"Escualo,"* one of Piazzolla's upbeat fugues. Like the shark it's named for, she increases her intensity. Falling easily into the role of the dragon-raised princess, she leans over him, licking and kissing and devouring. It's a mischievous piece and she enjoys teasing him, rubbing her fingers between his legs and lightly biting his nipples. He moans softly.

His hands rove along her spine and legs, pausing at the scars, knots and osteopathic deformities. Of course, he's an expert on the way bodies move, and she can see his mind working out ways to compensate. He sits up, crushing their bodies together, careful not to press too hard. "No more hiding," he whispers, and tugs off her slip.

Even on a cleared stage in front of empty chairs, there is a quiver of fear at losing this last piece of protection. She's no longer the woman who ran her own portion of the company, led meetings and presided over parties and benefit concerts. That part of her is still there, but it's long since been buried. For so long she believed herself lucky. Her face was unscathed. She could walk, after a fashion.

But the way Rafael traces the scars from both the surgeries and the accident tear open all the old hurt. She clings to him, breathing in the scent of his sweat, losing herself in the fact that he finds her strong and beautiful no matter her condition.

In *The Sleeping Prince*, the man deftly submits while at the same time taming the wild princess, showing her how to take pleasure in being the human woman she is. Rafael does the same. He gently gathers her into his arms, stands and twirls her around. The room spins faster and faster. She laughs in utter, childish delight, a sound she hasn't heard in far too long.

"*Milongueta,*" the next tune, is a piece that varies from pensive to passionate, much like a conversation. He is the guitar and she the piano, taking turns touching and admiring each other. He sets her down and sways his body, extending his limbs so she can see the length of him and admire his control. Every move he makes is practiced, and, she's sure, meant to heighten and arouse. He's a performer in every sense of the word, yet she senses a deeper part of him, the portion of his soul dedicated to serving others. Children. The impoverished.

Her. By celebrating her femininity rather than her disability, Rafael calms the soul that had grown feral from being alone for far too long.

When the music intensifies, she draws him close. His ass is taut and firm and she wastes no time in yanking his leggings down over his hips. Freed, his uncut cock juts forward and she takes in its thickness. Steadying her with one hand, he jerks his tights off and tosses them to the side of the stage. She grabs his balls, rolling them in her hands, relishing his expression as his mouth goes wide and his jaw trembles. He is hers completely.

They hold each other and he's careful not to move too fast or jerk her around. Instead he stretches her carefully, first in one direction and then another, limbering muscles wasted from forced bed rest. She aches, but it's bearable and far better than any physical therapy session. The pounding of her heart matches the music as it transforms into the driving rhythm of a more straightforward tango.

Like a child, she puts her feet on his and they move in unison, bending and swaying, his cock nudging enticingly between her legs. He turns her around so her back is to his chest. With nimble fingers he unclasps her bra and throws it aside just as the violin rises in a flourish.

In the dance, the performers only hint at sex, but she and Rafael have moved beyond that. He slides a hand down her belly, beneath her panties, and rubs her slick pussy until she's gasping and trembling against him. The music becomes a part of her, the ebb and flow of instruments guiding her body in reacting to his. She's aware only of him, his finger finding her entrance and plunging inside, his cock snug against her ass. She digs her fingernails into his arms, needing him now.

She shoves him down onto the chaise longue. He snatches off her panties then lifts her onto his lap. His cock is thick and hard in her hand, and she rubs him, enjoying the way he shudders and groans.

It isn't enough. She pushes him onto his back and tries to climb atop him, but her legs are stiff and weak and don't move where she wants them to. Rafael has more patience as well as stronger arms and gets her situated so she's straddling him. With his help she sinks down and he fills her.

At last she's on top, right where she wants to be, with the best view of his body and face. His hands are on her hips, guiding and supporting when she can't do it herself. The music continues to rise and fall, the instruments joined together just as their bodies are.

She loves him. Rafael. Her dancer.

And it's a joy to watch the way he pants as she takes him deep within her. He's wearing that look of fierce concentration, but he's stiff and quivering, panting hard in a way he never does while performing. She's pleased to be able to wring something new and previously unknown from his body. She wants to give him everything, so to the pounding of piano and bass she rides him hard, eliciting soft, sweet noises from his throat.

At last he grits his teeth and groans. His cock spasms, but that isn't what sends her over the edge into her own orgasm as the music hits its final crescendo. It's his expression, full of wonder, passion, pride...and love.

In late morning she wakes in her own room. Rafael has carried her there, put her to bed and vanished. The pain, too, has left. For the first time in a long while she can lie quietly and savor how good her body feels.

Besides, Rafael hasn't really left. He surrounds her, his love emanating from a hundred pictures. A new head shot sits atop the vacant pillow next to a copy of his itinerary. He's going home to Argentina and then he'll be back, and they will spend the night dancing.

MORE LIGHT

Laila Blake

Broken glass crunches under my feet, however carefully I try to move. I remembered to wear heavy boots; I'm not worried about getting hurt, but disturbing the silence in this place seems like a crime in itself. Like shouting in a church or jumping on a tomb. I almost want to hold my breath—first impressions are important. I look around, follow gilded stucco pillars up to a high, decorated ceiling. It might have borne a mural once, but all it has to show now is the natural water-painting of mold and stains, of moisture leaking through the visible cracks. It is eerily beautiful, and instinctively, I raise my camera but the lens is wrong. I need something far more light sensitive. Instead, I imagine the fabulous parties thrown here once upon a time; I see flapper dresses and thighs, energetic dancing, twinkling lights, and a small brass orchestra. In one of the dark corners, a couple could have stood, catching their breath, hands gliding under fabric. A shiver runs down my spine, and I am back to seeing dust and ruins.

Some shafts of sunlight manage to fall through the shattered windows; where the glass remains, though, the milky-gray grime of too many years shields against them all too effectively. I snap a picture of the infinitesimal dust particles glinting there, smile and follow the shaft of light through the viewfinder.

"You need these?" George calls from behind me. I jump at the volume and turn around. He was being manly, herding me away from the trunk so that he could carry in the equipment. Now, he is struggling to balance two lighting tripods.

"Definitely later," I say, nodding with a vague motion at the dim interior. "And the softbox and the reflectors," I add with a sheepish grin. I take the tripods off him and store them in a less photogenic corner, then I reach for the light meter in my bag and start to walk around the room again. His shouting seems to have shattered something and the atmosphere feels less sacred, less stifling. There is dust and crumbled debris everywhere.

George is the more finicky of the two of us—although, by long tradition, he would say that I am just messy. When he comes back, he carries a foldout table for the equipment, gives me a look and picks my bag up from the floor. He dusts it off and puts it on the table. I poke my tongue out at him and push middle and ring finger under my thumb in the universal rock-and-roll sign. He sighs, shakes his head and leaves for more stuff.

We were in college together. Back then, we just happened to hang with the same group of people—photography is impossible to do on your own. He was the handsome, jock type although he never played sports; he just looked like that with his tall physique and his naturally broad shoulders, the wavy dirty-blond hair. He still does. I was the chubby, nerdy one with the glasses and the shy, quiet voice, which I tried to make authoritatively deep. We weren't close but somehow we both ended up in Boston after college. His studio is just ten minutes away from mine and it's good to have friends who get it, friends who actually enjoy spending an hour driving around Connecticut to sneak into a long-abandoned building. Neither of us can afford an assistant.

I can hear him pottering around with the equipment behind me, but I'm still walking around, looking at the walls in the different rooms. From time to time, a little bit of dust falls from the ceiling and my heart beats a little faster. I try to be more graceful.

"First impression?" George asks coming up behind me. Less body conscious, he touches everything, hangs against the moldy doorjamb in a way I would never dare.

"There's something here," I say slowly and shrug. We both know that we've been to more impressively abandoned places, but this one has a solemn quality all its own that will be difficult to catch on camera. George hums in assent and we start to walk around, to try and find these special spots in which the natural light provides enough eerie illumination. Too much artificial light would ruin it, I think. I stroll back to the table and exchange my lens for a more light-sensitive one. It lies heavy in my hand and I almost drop it when I hear a loud crunching, dragging sound from somewhere in the bowels of the building. Just for a moment, I am sure this is when the zombies finally attack, but then I come back to reality, screw the lens on my camera and go to investigate.

George is dragging something over the floor, with a sound like a hundred tiny bells, and when he emerges from the shadow I see his broad grin and the ancient chandelier he's dug up from somewhere. It is dusty and broken in many places but it's still gorgeous, some herald of older times.

"Wow," I say—if just because it makes him grin with self-satisfaction as he gently drapes it into a shaft of sunlight.

We start shooting, find the best angle, the one that contrasts glittering light against squalor. My heart is beating faster; finally something is coming together.

If I wasn't used to George, he would be distracting to the point of annoyance. As it is, I smile and let him get on with his athleticism. I have long found that George just enjoys using his body—it makes him feel better about his photos. He crouches on the floor, then lies down completely, moving over the debris like a war-zone journalist through the sand. I am more stationary; I squat in place, fumble with the controls, find the perfect aperture settings. I am more given to placing the camera on the floor and snapping away with a remote than performing acrobatics. But I find myself momentarily entranced. From my vantage point, he is half hidden by the sparkling bits of polished glass and he stares at them with such a concentrated intensity, I just have to take a picture. He doesn't resist. Years of training and spending time with other photographers have ground photo shyness out of both of us. I find a different angle and click again, check the image on the screen. It is a beautiful portrait. I feel that rarely reoccurring flash of affection, the memory of a long-abandoned crush. When I let the camera sink, he smiles at me and returns the gesture, click, my thoughtful, aching face. I have that sudden childish urge to throw my hands in front of my face and launch myself in his direction to grab the camera and delete all evidence, but I stay there, squatting, hugging my knees for balance.

I give him a half smile instead and raise my camera. We regard each other through the viewfinders, only seeing shiny black surfaces where eyes and nose should be. Photography robots. The two clicks are almost simultaneous. Just like back in college.

"You know what would make this better?" he asks, carefully raising himself from the ground, mindful of the expensive equipment in his hand. I raise my brows, encourage him to go on.

"Nudity."

I snort and roll my eyes.

"Right, because the only real contribution women can make to photography is to take their clothes off..."

George just grins, above me now, my face at the level of his crotch, and he touches the tip of my nose. Just for a moment I want to be a different me, in a different body, and go right ahead. But then he shakes his head.

"You and your assumptions," he chides with that naughty schoolboy grin on his face. "Who said I was talking about you?"

My mouth falls open, just for a second, and my eyebrows seem intent on trying to disappear under my hairline. George laughs and offers me a hand to pull myself up from the floor. I accept. His hand is warm and I bite at the side of my lip, feeling lumpy in my long, shapeless sweater-dress and tights I'm wearing for comfort of movements.

"It would make good pictures," I agree, frowning as professionally as I can at the scenery. George seems satisfied. He hands me his camera and pulls his sweater over his head. It is a careless gesture only people with beautiful bodies, people without shame could be capable of. I place the strap of his camera around my neck and raise my own. In the first picture, he is unbuttoning his jeans; in the next he has pushed them to his knees. I snap the next of the curve of his back. In the shaft of lights, the tiny knobs of his spine are visible though his sleeveless shirt.

"I've always liked your portrait work," he says casually when he has finally liberated his jeans from his sneakers. My heart beats faster and I grin, not even capable of waving the compliment away.

"Thanks," I manage, and I catch that glimpse of stomach in the sun as he is pulling up his shirt. There is a fine light-brown line of hair that runs down into his tight boxer-briefs. It is just a shade darker than his hair. I exhale a shallow breath; send a prayer to the god of professionalism. But then he meets my eyes and he holds my gaze, fierce and serious in a way I have hardly ever seen him. I know he's pulling down his boxers but my eyes are arrested, held in place. Almost in panic, I throw my camera between us and manage a picture of that expression before it fades.

He doesn't cover himself; I wet my bottom lip and wordlessly direct him into the light. It throws beautifully stark shadows over his chest and face: planes of light and dark, all angles and masculinity only the magic of light and shadow can create. When I finally dare a glance at his crotch, I hardly manage to take it in before I tear my eyes away. He is not aroused—but I am. Tingling and nervous.

He looks like a god in the tiny preview screen. I ask him to pick up the chandelier and hold it up next to him: a hundred lights sparkle over his chest. I want to render these in black and white, I think—time in the studio will tell. I click, click, click—I can't get enough of the lights, of his body, his face. For long moments I get so lost in the work, I almost forget the aching tingly feeling between my legs but it always comes back, harder and more demanding than before.

Finally, I hand him back his camera, and he raises his brows questioningly as he sets the chandelier back onto the floor and shakes out his arm, tired from holding it up too long.

"Vulnerable photographer in dark corners," I tell him with a smile and bring a tripod, light and soft-box from the table.

"Still trying to be deep," he teases, and I want to blush, but I think I manage not to.

"Trying to be?" I ask instead, jokingly menacing where I don't feel like either. Not deep down. But he just looks at me for a moment too long and then starts to take pictures. He keeps the camera just far enough from his face to let me capture his expression, his natural body language. He is beautiful and I find myself envying his freedom. I catch him squatting by the chandelier, checking his setting, staring almost meditatively at the view-screen.

"Aren't you cold?" I finally ask. I never know how long I'm snapping away, but I finally caught a close-up of his shoulder and arm and I saw the gooseflesh rising there.

"Not very," he answers, but I think he's lying. I let my camera sink and take a deep breath. George is still watching me.

"What?" I finally ask.

He cocks up his chin, just once.

"Your turn."

For the second time, my jaw drops. This time I am more prepared for it. Raising any opposition isn't easy, and I take a deep breath.

"I'm not..." I start, but George interrupts me, before I can denigrate my looks, the state of my hair, or any of the million other imperfections I could name.

"You are," he says with a strange emphasis. "You really are." His eyes travel down my shoulder and along the side of my breast and he finally smiles. And there is something in his smile that has power and magic, especially in a place like this and without clothes to detract from his magnetism. I finally shrug as though I, too, think nothing of it. As though I do this all the time. I hand him my camera and try not to linger too long with my hands clinging to the hem of my long sweater.

"There'll be pressure marks all over," I warn ahead, then open my mouth again to say something else, something about my thighs or my stomach but then I don't.

"They'll plush out soon enough," he assures me, and I turn

around to pull the sweater over my face. I suck a sharp breath through my teeth at the cold against my skin. With my shoes, I clear a patch of ground and kick them off. Then I peel down my tights, my panties and finally reach back to open my bra. Unlike me, George grants me that moment of privacy. He is fumbling with the light and his settings. When he concentrates like this, a strand of hair falls into his face. His frown and the stance of his naked body suddenly take away from his jock appeal—he seems buffer in clothes but more handsome without them; he looks thoughtful and somehow *more*, deeper. I feel my chest flutter.

"Ready?" he asks, looking up at me. He comes around and picks my clothes up, then moves them out of frame. Out of reach. Wearing his sneakers but still nothing else, I notice that his cock is not quite as disinterested in the proceedings anymore, perking up as though in greeting. I feel more naked immediately and tear my eyes away, but also less nervous.

"Ready."

"Good, move against the window." His voice changes when he takes pictures. I have noticed that before. He is serious and intense. "Like that, look outside; place your hands on the window, careful where it's broken."

I try to take deep breaths; he tells me to relax and I do my best. Muscle by muscle I force the tension to flow out of my body.

"Ass too," he finally chides with a grin in his voice, and I have to laugh.

"Fuck you," I say, giggling, shake myself, and when I return to position he hums in assent. I can hear the camera shutter click and click. So fast, furiously clicking at every inch of my naked skin, the plush curve of my hip where it moves into the narrower waist. I turn toward him only a few degrees to let him catch just the hint of my breast. During those first poses, I feel torn between being all too conscious of my body, the extra softness, the lines and dimples over my ass—and my professional knowledge of taking pictures of women's bodies, and how to make them all believe in their own style of beauty. With time, I start to gravitate toward the latter. Moving slowly, I stretch myself, turn around and lean against the wall—grappling for courage I stare down the lens. A storm of clicks washes over me. The fear is starting to fade to exhilaration, adrenaline. We try more adventurous poses; I crouch in the dirt behind the chandelier, I rise up high to my toes, I turn around and touch my ass, my breasts. I place my chin on my shoulder and run my hands through my hair. I feel like one sore nerve ending, ready to explode at the smallest touch. Every once in a while he issues demands but for the most part, he seems happy to go along with my sudden sense of freedom.

When I take a break to stretch my arms out and rub them against the cold, George mounts his camera on a tripod, carefully sets the field and then nods at me to turn toward the wall. I hear the shutter click again, and again, and suddenly his hands encircle my waist. Another click—I hold my breath.

"You are beautiful," he whispers against my hair. *Click*. His teeth graze over my neck and I feel his cock pushing up against my ass. *Click, click*. Then he turns me around, and there is something in his eyes—seeking, wanting. I know that feeling, and for a moment seeing it in his eyes hits me like a slap across the face of an unconscious person. I wake up gasping for air and lean in to kiss him. He crosses the rest of the distance. *Click*. *Click*. I find the remote in his hand and take it from him; I can hardly breathe. His hands run down my arms and up my waist until his thumbs caress the undersides of my breasts. This time I release the shutter: *click*. *Click*. He walks me back a step; I find myself pressed against the wall, cool against my ass; then his hand is between my legs and my head falls back. *Click, moan, click.* With two fingers inside of me, the world grows hazier, I hardly think of the photos anymore, just know that the click sends tiny shoots of electricity through my body. I kiss his chest, his shoulders—he is so hard and tight under his skin, no softness like my body has in abundance. *Click.* Curling his fingers, he touches that perfect point inside me and I rise to my toes, aching, breathing, moaning. My tongue travels up his sternum; he tastes like salt and I want more. Soon I can't keep quiet and he lifts my leg over his hip. The angle is terrible but god, his cock feels good against my clit. *Click. Click.*

"A... around. Turn me around again," I moan, and his lips crash onto mine, hands grappling my face hard once more before he pushes me against the wall. My fingers find purchase, and I spread my legs. I can hear his aching sigh and suddenly, his hands push my ass apart and his tongue takes one long drag all the way from my clit up my crack. Fuck, fuck! He is fucking me with his tongue; I go cross-eyed for long heartbeats at a time and the grimy wall in front of me fades in and out of focus. A moment later he is inside of me. So full, so tight. His hand lands next to mine on the wall, and our fingers cross. We groan in unison, and he pushes his teeth into my neck. I almost forget: *click, click, click, click.*

The wall under my fingers is rough and he is digging his hand into my hip so hard it almost hurts, pushing into me again and again. With each thrust it feels like he's pressing every atom of air in my lungs, and each time I have to moan to let it out, or I might burst. And still I want more, more.

Slipping my hand between my legs, I find my clit and he sounds another groan. I return the remote; I need my hand to keep myself upright against the wall. Immediately the clicks storm faster, more aggressively; he seems to time two with each thrust: I am curled inward, rubbing, panting, greedy.

"I want you to come all over my cock," he breathes hot against my ear and I could cry it sounds so good. My body grants his wish less than a minute later, rearing, crying out and contracting all around him. He curses, groans and then pulls out. The splatter of his come lands on my ass and he whines like a wounded creature and collapses against my back. I shiver, find his hands and pull them more tightly around me.

"Hi," I whisper. It still sounds frighteningly loud in the silence. George moves his head, his lips brush against my shoulder and finally, he turns me around again. I hardly dare to look—but he's smiling.

"You're cold." His fingers trace my arms, then he rubs them a little ineffectually. We both feel gelatinous and tired.

"I didn't notice," I say, and grin. So does he. *Click*. We kiss. *Click, click*. He tastes even better now.

"Let's pack up... I want to get you somewhere warm. Somewhere with a bed."

I don't know what to say but I curl my arms around him; his hands find my ass again, smearing his come, and pull me against him. *Click*. Somewhere warm with a bed is exactly what we need.

THE SEVEN RAVENS

Ariel Graham

When she was born, the doctors came to Cecily's parents and told them not to expect their child to live. Her mother, still sweating and crying from labor, stared in horror at the managed care providers and tried to make herself understand. Her husband, shop clerk by day, wizard by night, went hard, his muscles tense, his jaw working as he started to chant.

"Don't," Cecily's mother said. "Please. She's just got here. Don't let her come into a world where you're—doing that." *Doing that* was her way around saying "magic" or "casting a spell." Cecily's mother didn't believe in magic. What Cecily's mother believed in was the small bundle of baby the doctors brought and placed in her trembling arms.

Cecily stared at her mother with pacific blue eyes. She'd been born with a hole in her heart, a condition that might heal, a condition that might not heal. Whatever her chances, the managed care providers had options and choices, and all of those options and choices came with price tags.

Cecily's father clenched his fists and tried hard to make money pour from the sky, or the cheap hospital silverware turn into gold, or for Cecily to heal spontaneously, but there are some things magic can't change.

They took her home with them, into the nursery they'd prepared with green baseboard and sky-blue walls, with yellow curtains like the sun and murals of birds flying. Cecily's father's best friend and his family, all of them raven haired and white skinned, lived next door, in an identical home in a cookie cutter subdivision. Cecily's father's best friend and his wife came to visit, bringing with them home-cooked meals, infant mobiles and the promise that someday, somehow, their families would unite. Through friendship. Or marriage.

For a week Cecily's parents lived in the wonder of Cecily, until the night her temperature rose, her cheeks flushing, her fists waving in infant fury.

"Send for a doctor," Cecily's mother said. "I don't want to move her. I don't want to take her out of the house." It was snowing outside, a deep January snow, the kind that erases streets and houses and buildings and leaves only white baffling that deadens voices and hope.

Cecily's father didn't want to leave Cecily's mother. He didn't want to leave his child's side. Terrified that his daughter would die, Cecily's father called his best friend and asked if he and his family would run and get help. If each went a to different source, their number of chances would increase.

"Help is coming," Cecily's father said to Cecily's mother when he went back into the nursery.

But help never came. Cecily's father's best friend's family panicked and lost their way in the snow. In their panic, they searched for hospitals and doctors but found closed restaurants and shuttered churches and abandoned gas stations. It was as if the snowstorm had changed the city into an unfamiliar, haunted place.

They returned without a doctor.

"We'll take a cab," Cecily's mother said, brushing past her husband with the baby swaddled in her arms. "Damn the out-of-program costs. I'm getting help."

Cecily's father agreed. His daughter had a hole in her heart. He had to do whatever he could to bring her fever down.

On the front porch, Cecily's father paused and stared up at the sky. There were birds overhead, wild and free as his daughter might never grow to be. He didn't know what had happened to his best friend's family, or why help never came, but he felt powerless and angry.

His wife turned back just before she reached the cab, the word *No* on her lips. Too late.

Cecily's father cursed his best friend's family, causing his children to take the form of ravens and not know the comfort of human society. In his panic, he misspoke the curse. His best friend's daughter was spared.

He followed his wife into the cab, ducking his head and sheltering his infant daughter from the snow.

Twenty-Four Years Later

On her twenty-fourth birthday, Cecily ran a marathon to prove she could. She celebrated with friends, with her family, and with her father's best friend's wife and daughter; her father's best friend had left the family years ago. Cecily had never known him.

"Where are you going?" her mother asked when Cecily started for the door just short of midnight. Even after twenty-four years, her mother worried.

"Just out to the porch for fresh air." Cecily was tall and blonde, beautiful and athletic. Tonight she was restless. Something had bothered her all day, something about the way her father's best friend's wife had watched her at her birthday dinner.

"Maybe she just thought it was weird I don't have a boyfriend," Cecily muttered to herself. She certainly thought it was odd, and something she'd like to rectify. She was twenty-four and groping in cars and meeting in college boys' filthy dorm rooms had gotten old. She wanted a boyfriend, a relationship and a life.

And she wanted something else. As she leaned against the porch rail, keeping neatly back out of the January snow, she let the desire build. For the last couple of years she'd dreamed of darkness.

Cecily shuddered in the dark. Even the cold couldn't stop her restless thoughts. In the dark, she imagined hands, touching her, hands that could touch any part of her. That could violate. Hands that could shame. Hands that would punish and spank and leave her naked and vulnerable. She imagined being tied, her hands pulled far from her breasts, her legs pulled far from each other. Powerless, she lay while faceless people stalked around her, touching, looking, laughing, filming. They held implements—dildos, vibrators, anal plugs, wooden spoons, hairbrushes, riding crops—and nothing she said could keep them from her. She had no will.

She'd given up her will. She'd consented.

The notion of consenting—to anything, to everything, to pain and pleasure, humiliation and punishment—left her weak. Breathless.

"Cecily?"

"Be right in, Dad."

But she wandered to the edge of the porch and stood a moment longer, staring into the darkness of the winter's night.

From the night around her came a voice. "Cecily."

She started. "Daddy?"

But she knew better.

"Cecily."

"Who are you?" Her heart pounded against her ribs, her breath came short, but she wasn't afraid. She was...curious. Certainly not hopeful. Of course her fantasies were only fantasies.

He stepped out of the pools of darkness that lay between the streetlights. He was tall, her father's age, his face lined with experience. Broad shoulders and somehow cunning hands. He moved those hands, and stardust fell from his fingers.

Cecily watched and saw a story begin to form.

"Once, you would not have been alone on this night. Our families were joined in friendship and tonight you would have been joined by boyfriend, friend, mentor, confidant, playmate, tormentor and lover."

She should be afraid, she thought. But standing in the dark, talking to a man she thought might be her father's long-lost best friend, she was only curious.

"I don't understand. I thought you only had a daughter?" Her father's best friend's daughter still lived next door with her father's best friend's ex-wife. She wasn't very nice, and Cecily had little to do with her.

"Now," he said. "Now I only have a daughter. But once I had more children." His voice held sorrow, and something else—a thrill of anger.

Cecily stepped forward instead of back, and put one hand on his arm. "Tell me," she said, and that is how Cecily learned that her father had cursed his best friend's family, turning young male restlessness into black winged ravens. Seven ravens, and seven keys which her father's best friend offered to Cecily on the flat of his hand. Seven keys that could break the curse.

One key opened a mountain of glass.

One key created a map.

One key led to heaven.

One key led to hell.

One key unlocked pleasure.

One key unlocked pain.

One key spoke the spell that would transform ravens back into humans, seven who might be Cecily's boyfriend, friend, mentor, confidant, playmate, tormentor and lover.

Each key came with a price.

She took the keys without question. She left the porch without thought. She went into the city in search of ravens.

The city was deserted. Another January snowstorm had caused a power failure and at midnight the streets were empty and impassable. Snow transformed the asphalt and concrete, the cars and buildings soft-edged and unreal. The snow muffled sound. No planes flew that night. No cars ran. No subways chugged. The streets were empty. Cecily's boots left tracks in the otherwise virgin snow.

She walked down the street, looking up at the snow that fell from the dull gray post-midnight sky. She carried the seven keys in her hands, wondering at the size and shape of them and what she was to do. Find a mountain made of glass, find a map, unlock heaven, unlock hell, learn pleasure and pain. Speak the spell that would release the ravens.

Snowflakes fell on her eyelashes and cheeks. She looked up toward the swirling sky and saw the mountain made of glass. The tallest building in the city, easily fifty stories tall, it glowed despite the power failure, all steel and glass, a seat of financial power.

She didn't question how she knew. She didn't know that she

was right. She just walked, heading for the building, the shiniest of the keys outstretched in her hand. Above her, seven ravens whirled in flight, following her down through the double glass doors into the marble lobby and into the shining steel elevator. She took the car up to the penthouse, stepped out into silence and glass and the city, dead and white below her. The room was full of white furniture and black birds.

"I'm here," Cecily said into the silence and from the darkness came a dark-haired man, hair black as coal, eyes dark as night. Six crows surrounded him, fluttering their midnight feathers, heads cocked to watch her with their oil-drop eyes.

He held his hand out to her with a low bow. "I am the son of your father's best friend. I would have been your boyfriend."

Cecily regarded him. "Do I know you?" She took his hand, let him draw her closer.

"You should."

His lips on hers were warm and soft. He smelled like feathers, warm and spicy. His hands went to her hair, cupped her face, slid down her back, then moved to her ass and pulled her tight against him. She felt his cock, hard against her, straining against the black slacks he wore, and her heart pounded faster.

Her clothes melted away as they might in a dream. The empty office was cold, and she shivered against him as he removed his clothes, letting them fall behind him. He pulled her to one of the white couches, guided her down beneath him. He caressed her breasts, letting his fingers trail out to her nipples, tweaking and pinching, laughing as she pulled away. He bit her neck and she breathed into him, aching for his touch, aching for something else.

His hands slipped down the slope of her hip bones, angled inward. One finger sank farther, touched her clit, slid between her lips. His breathing was rough and fast.

Cecily pressed against him, felt his cock against her naked belly, felt his fingers sinking into her cunt, probing, sliding, fucking her until her head fell back and her breathing all but stopped.

He pushed himself up on rigid arms, stared into her face, and he was familiar and a stranger, all at once.

"Spread your legs."

She blushed and moved them apart. He angled himself and sank deep inside her, his back arching as he pumped into her, hard, with very little rhythm, just need, as if he had missed her for so very many years.

Heat built in Cecily, warming her core, spreading from cunt and clit, spiraling up until she thought she'd burst with tension, with anticipation, and then she came for the first time with someone else there. Her head tipped back against the arm of the couch, and she screamed as waves of pleasure battered her.

"I would have been your boyfriend," he whispered in her ear and then he was gone, the ravens were gone, the room was empty and Cecily stood alone in the penthouse of the mountain of glass.

She pocketed the key and took the elevator back down to the marble lobby.

On the street again, she went looking for the map that would lead her to the son of her father's best friend, the one who would have been her friend.

Outside the glass and steel skyscraper she found the city map, a laminated and under-Plexiglas thing, battered despite protection, and seeming to indicate a city Cecily doubted resembled the one she was in.

The skeleton key in her hand fit the map stand, and when she opened it another map appeared, bright and primal and promising heaven.

He came up behind her, dark as his brother had been, and took her elbow.

"You shouldn't be out on the street at night," he said, guiding her toward a garden set between two of the steep buildings. There was little snow there, and the summerhouse was wound with morning glory vines. Six ravens followed them, swooping down to land noisily on the summerhouse roof, feathers twitching, beady eyes watching. Cecily felt warmer out of the never-ending snow.

"Do I know you?" He looked so like the man she had met before, the boyfriend, but of course they had to be brothers.

"I would have been your friend." His dark eyes were warm. He watched her, ready to laugh or cry at her desire.

"What's the price for knowing you now?"

"A kiss," he said, a Peter Pan request, and the ravens around them laughed rustily.

Cecily leaned up on her toes and kissed him on the cheek. The next instant he was gone.

She entered the summerhouse, her boots leaving snow on the steps to melt as spring triumphed over the January night. Inside, a black-haired, dark-eyed man stood watching her. His mouth quirked in a smile. He held one hand out to her, and Cecily took it, letting him lead her to a chaise swathed with silks. From somewhere she heard strains of music. She was warm and happy and unafraid.

One key unlocked heaven.

"Do I know you?" she asked. He looked like the boyfriend, and the friend. How many sons had her father's best friend had? No one had spoken of it in her house. No one had spoken of it in her father's best friend's ex-house.

"I would have been your mentor." He urged her down onto

the chaise, and when she struggled to stand again, he pressed her shoulders down, keeping her there.

"You have got to learn your place. You have got to learn."

Her cheeks burned as the stranger undressed himself, revealing alabaster skin, a lean chest, long arms, hard abs and finally a jutting cock, long and thick and hard for her. When she tried to turn her head away, tried to stand, he caught her face between his palms. Standing above her, he pressed his cock against her lips, pushing, guiding, forcing her mouth open.

Cecily's gaze rose to meet his. She opened her mouth and let him slide his length inside her. He tasted salty and musty, like deep-red wine, heated, with spices. He was already slick with precome, and when he pressed forward the head of his cock bumped the back of her throat.

"Open your throat. Let me in. Let me fuck you." He held the back of her head and rocked his hips into her. Cecily groaned, then let herself relax, opening to him, wrapping her tongue around his cock, sucking, hollowing her cheeks, letting him fill her as the fire between her legs grew again, not satiated. She wanted him; she wanted his hands, his cock, his tongue.

She wanted everything she'd had tonight, the sex, the friendship, the control.

The ravens watched from corners of the room, shifting noisily.

Cecily moved forward and back, sucking hard, feeling the man above her tense as he started to come. He pulled back suddenly, pulling himself free of her mouth. His come splattered across her face, into her hair.

"You're learning," he said, when she didn't reach up to wipe her mouth. "Go clean up." He pointed to a door in the back of the summerhouse. It hadn't been there when they'd entered. He followed her, at least as far as the door, which was locked. She fumbled with the seven keys in her hand, pulling one out that was a curious dull red, scorched by fire, perhaps.

One key leads to heaven. One would lead to hell.

The red key opened the door in the back of the summerhouse. The seven ravens swept through it with her, ruffling her hair, disturbing the air in the hot room. The door slammed shut behind her and Cecily knew without checking the door would be locked.

He stood in front of her, tall, strong, muscled, dark. He didn't smile, but held out his hand. The room around him was a stage set for play, the kind of thing she only let herself dream of in her most private moments.

Cecily's cheeks heated with shame. She wanted what was there.

One key would lead to hell.

"Do I know you?" she asked the muscular man. He had rolled up his sleeves over corded forearms and stood waiting for her. He looked so familiar, like a dream she might have had, or like the boyfriend, friend and mentor she had met.

"I would have been your confidant. Tell me your deepest fears. Your secrets." He whispered: "Your wants."

Her eyes swept the room. She wanted it all, the dungeon look, the exhibition, the pain, the punishment, the release. She wanted the crops and belts and canes and cats. She wanted him.

"I'm afraid."

"That's a good start."

He didn't offer her his hand again. Instead, he took hers roughly, yanked her to him, pulled her jeans down in a practiced motion and felt between her legs. "You're soaking wet. Smell yourself. Lick my fingers clean."

She tasted of onions, she thought, distracted, and came back to herself when he ordered her to strip. Around her the six ravens muttered and paced.

Her jeans, her panties, her T-shirt, her bra. Defenseless, she faced him, afraid, but wanting.

"Tell me what you fear the most."

She wouldn't, she thought, but her eyes betrayed her, darting fast across the room to fasten on the canes that hung from a peg.

In one fast motion he toppled her across a desk and Cecily thought now it looked like a schoolroom they were in; she wouldn't have been surprised to have a class sitting there watching, to find herself in tartan plaid, but it was just Cecily, naked, vulnerable, watched by the ravens.

"Don't move."

She heard him cross the room. Her breath caught. She held it. This was what she'd waited for.

This was what she'd feared.

It took forever for him to cross the small space, to bring back one of the thin, whippy canes and one of the thick, formidable ones.

She wanted him to make her count. In her darkest moments, she thought the humiliation of keeping her own count would be—sublime? Hellish? Hers.

He was to have been her confidant. Of course he knew.

"Count," he ordered, and then he started. The thick cane cracked down across her ass, hitting the sweet spot. Cecily shouted in surprise and pain, bucked up and felt him shove her back down hard. The sting blossomed and an instant later became searing, red-hot pain.

"Count!" he shouted.

"One!"

"Sir."

"One, Sir!"

The thick cane again, leaving a trail of red; she could feel welts starting and welts over welts. She cried, she kicked; six times the cane descended and then he stopped.

She felt him walk close behind her. His hands came down, mauling her ass, pinching handfuls of reddened, angry flesh. One hand reached down between her legs.

"You're even wetter."

She moaned.

"Six more." And the cane snapped across her skin, leaving marks, leaving trails. She hurt. She screamed. She struggled even as the ravens laughed. Under it all, the need crested, the pleasure built, the pain exploded until Cecily exploded, clit throbbing, cunt pulsing, mouth open as she panted through the orgasm.

He hit her one more time as it faded. She grunted, let her head drop to the desk.

The snow woke her instants later. Snow blowing into the room, chasing away the warmth of heaven, the heat of hell. She wasn't surprised to find herself dressed again. She ached, warmth spreading from her ass to her cunt and clit. She wanted more.

The seven ravens watched her. Another key would lead her to pleasure. Out, then, from the hellish room. There was only one door, and it wasn't the one she'd come in through. She crossed to it, finding a slim silver key that fit the lock. The ravens brushed through ahead of her. Cecily followed and stood in a huge room full of people milling about. Instantly she glanced down at herself, but her clothes were still there, jeans and a T-shirt, boots and keys. She searched then, until she found him.

He was grinning, mischievous and cute, with sharper features than the others, but just as dark of hair, pale of skin, just as tall and strong and just as much in control of Cecily.

She wanted to say she'd already figured it out this time but her mouth shaped the words. "Do I know you?"

"I would have been your playmate."

She thought initially that would have meant something else. Now she just took his hand and allowed him to lead her up onto a stage at the end of the room. Now the guests in the room turned and looked at the ravens fluttering above them, then up to the stage where Cecily's playmate removed her clothes.

"Show them," he said.

She stared at him, her hands protectively over breasts, legs twisting together.

He laughed at her. "Oh, no. No." He took her hands away from herself and walked her into the lights at the edge of the stage. Standing behind her he offered up her breasts to the crowd, pushed her hips forward and separated her lips, turned her and bent her and spread her legs and all the while the guests assembled sipped their drinks and petted each other and laughed and commented and asked if they could touch.

"No," her playmate said. "She's all mine."

His touch tickled. He stroked and nipped, he kissed and licked, he squeezed her aching ass and slid a finger into her asshole and wouldn't let her go when she tried to squirm away. He tickled her and stoked her and bit her and told her she was beautiful and the fire inside her climbed again. Cecily fed off the crowd, ashamed and frightened and excited and abandoned. She reached down for his cock, hard inside his black slacks, rubbed him hard and laughed when he pushed her away, went right back to it until he turned her, tucked her butt into his crotch, bent her and reached his arms around to play with her clit.

"Come. Come for the nice people. Let them see your face when I make you come."

Cecily screamed, head dropping, her entire body convulsing.

She heard the guests laugh, some of them applaud; she heard groans and sighs as the assembled personages lost their clothes and their minds and pleasure rippled through the room.

"I want to stay here," Cecily said, eyeing the ravens. Five of them circled.

"I won't let you," her tormentor said, tearing her from the arms of her playmate. He forced her fingers around the spiky iron key and dragged her to the door across the stage, the one that lead to pain.

A plain, utilitarian room, where six ravens circled, cawing. Cecily shrank back. In the center of the room stood the bed, four poster, empty of covers, only rough rope ties on the posts. He dragged her to it, threw her down faceup, grabbed her arms and legs and tied her. Struggling did no good. He was stronger. He was impossibly faster.

"Please!" Cecily begged her tormentor as the fire inside her grew again. This had been one of the dark dreams. This had been the hidden shameful fantasy. This had been the want, the need, the desire. The question. Could she?

And now, this was the reality.

He held a cane: slim, black, long. Held it for her to see, laughed as she watched when he brought it down slowly and dipped it into her cunt. Her juices coated it. Her clit throbbed, aching for touch. Her cunt pulsed at the tip of the cane.

He laughed, and lifted the cane, and brought it down across her nipples.

Cecily screamed in pain as sting became burn.

And burn became pleasure.

And pleasure became pain again. He struck her thighs, her breasts, her mons. He laughed as she cried, and laughed as she squirmed, and laughed when he pushed the cane between her legs, and let her ride it until she screamed again, this time coming.

He left her there, tied spread-eagled, sweating and shaking, crying a little, until the pain and pleasure both ebbed and then he unknotted the ropes and let her stand.

She wasn't dressed this time. She didn't care. There was only one key left, a black one shaped like a raven's wing. She carried it with her across the room, stumbling a little, making little cries of want and fear. She stopped at the black barred door of heavy wooden timbers, iron marking the shape of a raven across it.

One key led to the spell that would transform raven to human, and now she might find boyfriend, friend, mentor, confidant, playmate, tormentor and lover.

Seven ravens flew in over her head. The room looked like her parents' living room in the house she had grown up in, the house next door to her father's best friend's house where he'd lived with his wife and daughter. But once, he'd said, he'd had more children. Seven sons? Or only one?

The key would fit the front door that led to the porch where her father had stood when he cursed his best friend's children. When she turned it, the door opened to snow and darkness. Here she would find the spell.

She didn't know what the spell was. Didn't know what she was supposed to find.

But her father had cursed them.

Cecily blessed them.

"Blessed be."

There was a ruffle of feather behind her at the entrance to the house. Cecily turned slowly to see the seven dark haired men standing in the doorway. One would be her lover.

The seventh stepped forward and held out his hand.

Cecily reached for him and one after another the seven fell into a line, each so hard on the heels of the one before him they seemed to be tumbling together like dominos, not knocking into each other but falling inside each other, these raven-haired men who looked so alike.

Cecily's father's best friend had said he had more children, not how many more. She held her breath, childish and wanting the boyfriend, friend, mentor, confidant, playmate, tormentor and lover.

He stood before her, one man, dark hair, pale skin. He held his hand out to her and there was no door to go through, no key to unlock secrets, turn curses. They were together, and the curse was breaking.

There was one man, one father's best friend's son.

"Are you the one I've been waiting for?" she asked. The question sounded naïve to her own ears, but what could she do other than ask?

The raven-haired man pulled her close, his embrace a combination of need and want, request and demand. He held her as if she were precious and with a fierce roughness that sent her heart racing.

"I've been waiting for you," he said.

Cecily frowned. "There were seven," Cecily said, uncertain if she felt afraid or greedy or hopeful.

"Friend, boyfriend, mentor, confidant, playmate, tormentor, lover. What use is a husband who is not all those things?"

Cecily tilted her head and studied him. The night passing behind them seemed a dream, but she remembered it clearly. "Seven ravens," she said. "Seven sons, seven keys."

"Seven aspects," he corrected.

They were alone in the house, all seven rooms to themselves.

"Let me show you," her friend said. He took her hand and led her to the bedroom, and there his kiss trapped her mouth under his, hot and intimate as the boyfriend held her, stroking her hair, whispering to her.

Cecily let her head fall back, let him hold her as he tugged at her clothes, laughing when he tangled her in her T-shirt and bra. Her boyfriend kissed her neck and bit her ears and whispered what he wanted to do to her.

Cecily felt molten, wet and wild; her hands stroked him through his jeans. His cock was hard and familiar. She wanted him, now, and she willingly complied when her mentor told her what he wanted.

"Down on your knees, don't use your hands." He freed himself from the button-fly jeans, his cock rigid, straining toward her. She opened her lips, let him press between them. He was salty and silky in her mouth, huge and forceful and Cecily gave herself over to instruction, to his hands that pressed her head against him, to his words, low and throaty, telling her to take it deep. She hollowed her cheeks, sucked and let her tongue play, and when he came, filling her mouth, she swallowed and gasped and let her confidant pull her to her feet.

"That's what you like, isn't it?" he asked. "Being controlled? Nothing left up to you? Nothing you could do about it? Tell me."

She leaned close to him, tumbling them both down to the huge arctic bed, all white jersey sheets and white microfiber blankets, white as the snow that filled the world on her birthday.

"I want it," she said. "I want all of it. I want everything. I want to do everything. I want to be told."

"Everything?" her playmate asked, and pulled her on top of him, hands exploring, teasing feathery fingertip touches along the insides of her hip bones and along her lips, down into her wet folds. He pulled her up to straddle him, the two of them sideways on the enormous white bed, and slid deep inside her.

Cecily gasped, her eyes closing.

"Do you like this?" her playmate asked, fingertips brushing down the slope of her breasts.

She nodded, inarticulate.

"Do you like this?" her tormentor asked, his fingers tightening, tweaking, pulling, stretching her nipples until she made another sound, of pain and want.

"Tell me." He bit her breast. "Tell me." An open-handed slap across her ass as she rode him.

"Tell me." As the two of them came together, Cecily and her lover, in the arctic bed as the snow fell outside the house, the curse lifted.

ABOUT THE AUTHORS

VALERIE ALEXANDER (valeriealexander.org) lives in Arizona. Her work has previously been published in *Best of Best Women's Erotica*, *Best Bondage Erotica* and other anthologies.

DANI BAUTER spends her days working as a marketing and events coordinator at an independent bookstore. She has had book reviews published in *Elle Magazine* and stories published in *Viscera* edited by Cara Bruce and *Book Lovers: Sexy Stories from Under the Covers* edited by Shawna Kenney.

LAILA BLAKE (lailablake.com) is an author, linguist and translator. She writes character-driven love stories; blogs about writing, feminism and society; and cofounded the small publishing venture Lilt Literary.

EVEY BRETT is a writer of erotica and paranormal romance. She has a degree in Writing Popular Fiction from Seton Hill

University and has attended the Lambda Writers Retreat for Emerging LGBT voices. She lives in Southern Arizona with two cats, a snake and her Lipizzan mare, Carrma.

RACHEL KRAMER BUSSEL (rachelkramerbussel.com) is the editor of *Please, Sir; Yes, Sir; He's on Top; Cheeky Spanking Stories; Spanked; Bottoms Up; Anything for You: Erotica for Kinky Couples; Twice the Pleasure: Bisexual Women's Erotica; Baby Got Back: Anal Erotica; Best Bondage Erotica 2011, 2012, 2013* and many other erotica anthologies.

One day, **SUE LENÈE CIX,** strapped for cash, found a side job as an erotic ghostwriter. She foregrounds communication and consent, bisexuality, thought, metaphor, and character-driven sexploration. She is currently at work on a short story collection centered around bisexuality and the ocean, and an erotic science fiction novel.

BEATRIX ELLROY is a book hound with a love of words, the dirtier the better. She's a recent entrant into the world of erotica writing. Previous work has included everything from articles about computer games to literary fiction to academic journal articles, but erotica is her passion and her weakness.

TAMSIN FLOWERS (tamsinflowers.com) loves to write light-hearted erotica, often with a twist in the tail/tale and a sense of fun. Her stories have appeared in a wide variety of anthologies for publishers including Cleis Press, Xcite Books, House of Erotica and Go Deeper Press. She has now graduated to novellas and a novel.

LANA FOX (lanafox.com) is cofounder of Go Deeper Press and she co-runs the indie publishing service Here Booky Booky. Fox is the author of the novel *Confessions of a Kinky Divorcée* and has appeared in many erotic collections, including *Best Women's Erotica, Alison's Wonderland, Best Bondage Erotica* and *Dream Lover.*

ARIEL GRAHAM is a Reno native who is happiest surrounded by sagebrush and sunshine. She shares her home with her husband and a pack of felines. Ariel's work has appeared in *Best Lesbian Romance; Please, Sir* and *Please, Ma'am* and in online magazines like *Oysters & Chocolate* and *Clean Sheets.*

LYDIA HILL is published in the erotic romance anthologies *Words of Lust, My First Threesome* and *Slave for Love.*

MALIN JAMES's (malinjames.com) erotica has appeared in anthologies from Cleis Press, Xcite Books and Burning Book Press, including *Best Men's Erotica 2014, The Mammoth Book of Urban Erotic Confessions* and the bestselling *The Big Book of Orgasms: 69 Sexy Stories.* She is currently working on her first erotic novel.

GWENDOLYN KANSEN is a writer and art student in New York City who has written for *Thought Catalog, The Frisky, Erotic Review Magazine* and *Flurt.* She once ran a sex humor site on the People of Walmart network, but now finds vulnerable stories about the sex lives of outsiders more interesting.

ANNABETH LEONG (annabetherotica.com) has written erotica for more than forty anthologies, including *Best Bondage Erotica 2013* and *2014* and *Best Erotic Romance 2014.* She has written a number of erotic novels for Ellora's Cave and Breathless Press. Her most recent novel, *Untouched,* is published by Sweetmeats Press. She lives in Providence, RI.

JT LOUDER writes queer porn under a male pseudonym (Jacob Louder) and really hopes you like it. Find more of their work at godeeperpress.com.

Award-winning erotica writer **GISELLE RENARDE** is a queer Canadian, avid volunteer, contributor to more than one hundred short-story anthologies and author of numerous electronic and print books, including *Anonymous, Nanny State* and *My Mistress' Thighs.* Ms. Renarde lives across from a park with two bilingual cats who sleep on her head.

ALISON TYLER (alisontyler.blogspot.com) is the editor of fifty anthologies for Cleis Press, including *Twisted* and *The Big Book of Bondage.* Her novellas have been published by Harlequin, Go Deeper Press and Pretty Things Press. *Dark Secret Love,* her meta-novel, recently won the Gold Ippy Award for Erotica.

RACHEL WOE is a writer/artist who probably watched too many R-rated movies as a youngster. A longtime lover of erotic fiction, she used to bring *Story of O* and *The Sleeping Beauty Trilogy* to school, folded inside brown paper covers. She is a University of Vermont graduate residing in New England.

ABOUT THE EDITOR

MS. VIOLET BLUE (@violetblue, tinynibbles.com) is an investigative tech reporter at CNET, Zero Day, ZDNet, and CBS News, as well as an award-winning sex author and columnist, making her the foremost expert in the field of sex and technology. She travels to hacker conferences and hacker gatherings around the world to cover hacking, cybercrime and personal privacy violations in countries such as Malaysia, Germany, Morocco, China, the Dominican Republic, the United States and Serbia. In 2012, Blue presented "Hackers as a High-Risk Population," bringing harm reduction to the featured stage for CCC's twenty-ninth hacker conference in Hamburg. She is an Advisor to Without My Consent, a Member of the Internet Press Guild, a Member of the Center for Investigative Reporting, and is an Editor on the Board for Routledge's Porn Studies Journal.

Blue has appeared on CNN and "The Oprah Winfrey Show" and is regularly interviewed, quoted and featured in a variety of publications that includes ABC News and the *Wall Street Journal*.

She has authored and edited award-winning, bestselling books in eight translations—one is excerpted on Oprah Winfrey's website—and has been a sex columnist for the *San Francisco Chronicle*. She has been at the center of many Internet scandals, including Google's "nymwars" and Libya's web domain censorship and seizures. Forbes calls her "omnipresent on the web" and named her a Forbes Web Celeb. She has given keynote talks at such conferences as ETech, LeWeb, and the Forbes Brand Leadership Conference, she received a standing ovation at Seattle's Gnomedex, and she has given two Tech Talks at Google.

Best Erotica Series

Happy Endings Forever and Ever

Many More than Fifty Shades of Erotica

Please, Sir
Erotic Stories of Female Submission
Edited by Rachel Kramer Bussel

If you liked *Fifty Shades of Grey*, you'll love the explosive stories of *Please, Sir*. These damsels delight in the pleasures of taking risks to be rewarded by the men who know their deepest desires. Find out why nothing is as hot as the power of the words "Please, Sir."
ISBN 978-1-57344-389-0 $14.95

Yes, Sir
Erotic Stories of Female Submission
Edited by Rachel Kramer Bussel

Bound, gagged or spanked—or controlled with just a glance—these lucky women experience the breathtaking thrills of sexual submission. *Yes, Sir* shows that pleasure is best when dispensed by a firm hand.
ISBN 978-1-57344-310-4 $15.95

He's on Top
Erotic Stories of Male Dominance and Female Submission
Edited by Rachel Kramer Bussel

As true tops, the bossy hunks in these stories understand that BDSM is about exulting in power that is freely yielded. These kinky stories celebrate women who know exactly what they want.
ISBN 978-1-57344-270-1 $14.95

Best Bondage Erotica 2013
Edited by Rachel Kramer Bussel

Let *Best Bondage Erotica 2013* be your kinky playbook to erotic restraint—from silk ties and rope to shiny cuffs, blindfolds and so much more. These stories of forbidden desire will captivate, shock and arouse you.
ISBN 978-1-57344-897-0 $15.95

Luscious
Stories of Anal Eroticism
Edited by Alison Tyler

Discover all the erotic possibilities that exist between the sheets and between the cheeks in this daring collection. "Alison Tyler is an author to rely on for steamy, sexy page turners! Try her!"—Powell's Books
ISBN 978-1-57344-760-7 $15.95

Bestselling Erotica for Couples

Sweet Life
Erotic Fantasies for Couples
Edited by Violet Blue

Your ticket to a front row seat for first-time spankings, breathtaking role-playing scenes, sex parties, women who strap it on and men who love to take it, not to mention threesomes of every combination.
ISBN 978-1-57344-133-9 $14.95

Sweet Life 2
Erotic Fantasies for Couples
Edited by Violet Blue

"This is a we-did-it-you-can-too anthology of real couples playing out their fantasies."
—Lou Paget, author of *365 Days of Sensational Sex*
ISBN 978-1-57344-167-4 $15.95

Sweet Love
Erotic Fantasies for Couples
Edited by Violet Blue

"If you ever get a chance to try out your number-one fantasies in real life—and I assure you, there will be more than one—say yes. It's well worth it. May this book, its adventurous authors, and the daring and satisfied characters be your guiding inspiration."—Violet Blue
ISBN 978-1-57344-381-4 $14.95

Afternoon Delight
Erotica for Couples
Edited by Alison Tyler

"Alison Tyler evokes a world of heady sensuality where fantasies are fearlessly explored and dreams gloriously realized."
—Barbara Pizio, Executive Editor, *Penthouse Variations*
ISBN 978-1-57344-341-8 $14.95

Three-Way
Erotic Stories
Edited by Alison Tyler

"Three means more of everything. Maybe I'm greedy, but when it comes to sex, I like more. More fingers. More tongues. More limbs. More tangling and wrestling on the mattress."
ISBN 978-1-57344-193-3 $15.95

Red Hot Erotic Romance

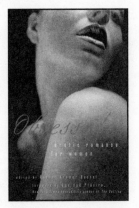

Obsessed
Erotic Romance for Women
Edited by Rachel Kramer Bussel

These stories sizzle with the kind of obsession that is fueled by our deepest desires, the ones that hold couples together, the ones that haunt us and don't let go. Whether just-blooming passions, rekindled sparks or reinvented relationships, these lovers put the object of their obsession first.
ISBN 978-1-57344-718-8 $14.95

Passion
Erotic Romance for Women
Edited by Rachel Kramer Bussel

Love and sex have always been intimately intertwined—and *Passion* shows just how delicious the possibilities are when they mingle in this sensual collection edited by award-winning author Rachel Kramer Bussel.
ISBN 978-1-57344-415-6 $14.95

Girls Who Bite
Lesbian Vampire Erotica
Edited by Delilah Devlin

Bestselling romance writer Delilah Devlin and her contributors add fresh girl-on-girl blood to the pantheon of the paranormal. The stories in *Girls Who Bite* are varied, unexpected, and soul-scorching.
ISBN 978-1-57344-715-7 $14.95

Irresistible
Erotic Romance for Couples
Edited by Rachel Kramer Bussel

This prolific editor has gathered the most popular fantasies and created a sizzling, no-holds-barred collection of explicit encounters in which couples turn their deepest desires into reality.
978-1-57344-762-1 $14.95

Heat Wave
Hot, Hot, Hot Erotica
Edited by Alison Tyler

What could be sexier or more seductive than bare, sun-warmed skin? Bestselling erotica author Alison Tyler gathers explicit stories of summer sex bursting with the sweet eroticism of swimsuits, sprinklers, and ripe strawberries.
ISBN 978-1-57344-710-2 $15.95

Read the Very Best in Erotica

Fairy Tale Lust
Erotic Fantasies for Women
Edited by Kristina Wright
Foreword by Angela Knight

Award-winning novelist and top erotica writer Kristina Wright goes over the river and through the woods to find the sexiest fairy tales ever written.
ISBN 978-1-57344-397-5 $14.95

In Sleeping Beauty's Bed
Erotic Fairy Tales
By Mitzi Szereto

"Classic fairy tale characters like Rapunzel, Little Red Riding Hood, Cinderella, and Sleeping Beauty, just to name a few, are brought back to life in Mitzi Szereto's delightful collection of erotic fairy tales."
—Nancy Madore, author of *Enchanted: Erotic Bedtime Stories for Women*
ISBN 978-1-57344-376-8 $16.95

Frenzy
60 Stories of Sudden Sex
Edited by Alison Tyler

"Toss out the roses and box of candies. This isn't a prolonged seduction. This is slammed against the wall in an alleyway sex, and it's all that much hotter for it."
—Erotica Readers & Writers Association
ISBN 978-1-57344-331-9 $14.95

Fast Girls
Erotica for Women
Edited by Rachel Kramer Bussel

Fast Girls celebrates the girl with a reputation, the girl who goes all the way, and the girl who doesn't know how to say "no."
ISBN 978-1-57344-384-5 $14.95

Can't Help the Way That I Feel
Sultry Stories of African American Love, Lust and Fantasy
Edited by Lori Bryant-Woolridge

Some temptations are just too tantalizing to ignore in this collection of delicious stories edited by Emmy award-winning and *Essence* bestselling author Lori Bryant-Woolridge.
ISBN 978-1-57344-386-9 $14.95

Unleash Your Favorite Fantasies

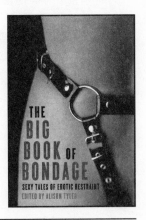

Ordering is easy! Call us toll free or fax us to place your MC/VISA order.
You can also mail the order form below with payment to:
Cleis Press, 2246 Sixth St., Berkeley, CA 94710.

ORDER FORM

QTY	TITLE	PRICE
___	_____	___
___	_____	___
___	_____	___
___	_____	___
___	_____	___
___	_____	___
___	_____	___
___	_____	___

SUBTOTAL _____

SHIPPING _____

SALES TAX _____

TOTAL _____

Add $3.95 postage/handling for the first book ordered and $1.00 for each additional book. Outside North America, please contact us for shipping rates. California residents add 9% sales tax. Payment in U.S. dollars only.

* Free book of equal or lesser value. Shipping and applicable sales tax extra.

Cleis Press • Phone: (800) 780-2279 • Fax: (510) 845-8001
orders@cleispress.com • www.cleispress.com
You'll find more great books on our website

Follow us on Twitter @cleispress • Friend/fan us on Facebook